$\mathcal{P}$lum stopped when she reached Taylor. "Oh, Taylor. Did you hear? Gypsy Trails is having a show."

"Yeah. I heard," Taylor said flatly as she loosened Mandy's cinch.

"Great! I guess I'll be seeing you in the *beginner* class then, when I win a blue. It's okay, you can cheer for me."

"You're not a beginner, Plum. Why don't you let *real* beginners have a chance? It's just so you can win, isn't it?"

"It's always fun to win," Plum cooed.

"You don't *always* win," Taylor reminded her.

"I don't know *what* you're talking about," Plum replied.

Ride over to
WILDWOOD STABLES

WILDWOOD STABLES

Stealing the Prize

BY SUZANNE WEYN

SCHOLASTIC INC.

New York   Toronto   London   Auckland
Sydney   Mexico City   New Delhi   Hong Kong

ISBN 978-0-545-23091-9

12 11 10 9 8 7 6 5 4 3 2   10 11 12 13 14 15/0

Printed in the U.S.A.   40
First printing, November 2010

For **Diana Gonzalez** with thanks for all her creative and informational contributions to this story.

Chapter 1

Taylor Henry stroked Prince Albert's silky black muzzle as she fitted a soft snaffle-bit bridle over his head.

"The County HORSE people will be here any minute now, so you have to be on your best behavior," she reminded the all-black quarter horse gelding. "Whatever rider they want you to carry, just do it. Don't be difficult. These will be mostly first-time riders. Some of them might even be scared of horses."

Taylor quickly tied back her brown, shoulder-length hair. "It's not so bad," she added in her gentlest tone. "Other horses do it all the time."

Prince Albert sputtered, which made Taylor smile. She loved the way he always made some sound when he was spoken to. Taylor knew he was probably just responding to her voice, but she still liked to imagine that he understood her and was replying in his own horse language. It seemed possible that a quarter horse could really do this — it was such a smart, people-friendly breed.

"Don't argue," she said, speaking as if Prince Albert had really objected. She clipped the reins to the ring at the side of the halter. "We've been over this plenty of times."

County HORSE was Pheasant County's therapeutic riding program. HORSE stood for Health Office Rehabilitative Services, Equestrian. The program was designed to help people with various physical and psychological disabilities by providing them with the benefits of horseback riding.

Before the ranch got the County HORSE contract, there had been only one therapeutic student at Wildwood Stables, a seven-year-old girl with autism named Dana. She and Prince Albert had competed in the Rotary Horse Show's therapeutic riding event a few months earlier. Prince Albert's calm, gentle performance had not only won him a ribbon as Best Therapeutic Horse, it also convinced the County HORSE people to run their program at Wildwood.

Winning the much-needed business for the ranch was Taylor's proudest accomplishment. She felt it proved that even though, at thirteen, she was the youngest and least experienced member of the all-volunteer staff, she was a valuable contributor. And — maybe even more importantly — it underscored Prince Albert's value to Wildwood Stables.

After placing a striped pad and an all-purpose saddle on Prince Albert's sturdy back and tightening the girth, Taylor moved to the stall next to his.

"How are you today, Pixie?" she greeted Prince Albert's best friend, a cream-colored Shetland pony mare. She stroked the pony's wild, fuzzy blonde mane. "Good news. You're coming out, too. We're going to need every horse available today. You and Prince Albert can stay together all through the lesson. I know you'll like that, won't you?"

Taylor began tacking up the small pony. Pixie would be useful today in more ways than one. For one thing, since the ranch had started using Pixie for pony rides, she had proven that she was patient with children. Even a crying toddler didn't seem to upset her.

"You show Prince Albert how it's done today, okay,

Pixie?" Taylor said as she tightened the girth under Pixie's belly.

Taylor hoped the pony's good example would inspire the gelding. She couldn't count on that, though. So far, Prince Albert had allowed only two riders on his back: Taylor and Dana. He had let Taylor ride him from the start, and he clearly wanted to be a one-girl horse. Taylor would have adored that, too, but it simply wasn't an option. The deal she had struck with Wildwood Stables was that Prince Albert and Pixie could be used as school and trail horses in exchange for their board. If Prince Albert didn't cooperate with this plan, Mrs. LeFleur, who owned the struggling ranch, couldn't afford to keep him.

Despite his royal name, *Prince* Albert needed to work for his food and shelter. Without this arrangement, Taylor's family couldn't pay for his upkeep, either.

And so far, Prince Albert had *not* been particularly cooperative. The one exception to this was Dana. After some initial resistance, Prince Albert had allowed the delicate girl to ride him. To Taylor, that was a huge triumph — but unfortunately it was one that hadn't been repeated with any other riders yet.

From across the stable's wide aisle, tall and graceful Daphne Chang led her gray speckled mare, Mandy, out of the stall. With a whinny of enthusiasm, the sturdy barb-Arabian mix tossed her black mane as she took in a cool breeze wafting through the open stable door.

The ranch's sixteen-year-old riding instructor was dressed somewhat casually in black half chaps, a hooded sweatshirt, and ankle-high paddock boots. Her silky long black hair was tied back, and she held an olive green brimmed hunt cap helmet in her hand.

Daphne stopped in front of Pixie's stall, holding Mandy by a lead line. "I've saddled Cody," she said, referring to the spotted Colorado Ranger gelding that boarded at Wildwood and that the ranch had permission to use. "He's in the front corral already."

"Okay," Taylor answered. "Are we using Shafir?"

"I don't think we should," Daphne replied. "I didn't tack her up. She's still too unpredictable."

"You're probably right," Taylor agreed. Wildwood's young mare was frisky and playful, a trait Arabians were noted for, and she'd only recently been brought along far enough in her training to be ridden. "I hope we have enough horses, though," Taylor added, chewing her right thumbnail anxiously, a habit she found impossible to resist in stressful times.

"Are you nervous about today?" Daphne asked.

"There's a lot to worry about," Taylor said. "Don't you think so?"

Daphne cocked her head to the side. "Like what?"

"I don't know," Taylor said. "Couldn't a million things go wrong? There might be more students than we can handle. Someone might get hurt. And . . . and . . ."

"And Prince Albert might not let anyone on his back," Daphne finished Taylor's unspoken sentence.

Taylor sighed forlornly. "Yeah . . . and that."

"That's what you're *really* concerned about, isn't it?"

"I guess so," Taylor admitted.

"Don't worry. I think it'll be all right."

Taylor brightened at Daphne's words. "You do? Why?"

Smiling, Daphne shrugged. "It's a sunny day, much warmer than it usually is at the end of November. Wildwood has this great new business. I'm just feeling optimistic."

"Oh," Taylor said, disappointed. She'd hoped that Daphne had some sound equestrian information on which to base her idea that Prince Albert would do the right thing, some wise observation taken from her impressive knowledge of horses — not just wishful thinking and a good mood!

"Think positive," Daphne advised cheerfully, leading Mandy toward the stable's wide opening. "Mrs. LeFleur will help, too. It'll all be fine. See you outside."

Taylor sighed once more. "Think positive," she murmured as she ran the brush back through Pixie's wild mane, echoing the words with much less conviction than Daphne had used. Taylor supposed it was good advice. Besides, what other choice did she have?

She led Pixie into the aisle, then went into Prince Albert's stall and took him out. "Come on, you guys. It's time." Taylor clipped a lead line to the side strap of Prince Albert's bridle and began to walk him out of the stable, confident that Pixie would follow wherever Prince Albert went.

As she walked them forward, Taylor heard a sound coming from the back entrance of the stable. A slim girl with long, nearly black curls stepped into the aisle. "I came to help," said Mercedes Gonzalez, striding purposefully toward Taylor.

"I thought you weren't supposed to be here," Taylor said, a little surprised to see her friend.

"I know — and *you* know that I couldn't care less," Mercedes replied with brazen confidence.

"But what if your mother finds out?" Taylor asked.

Mercedes shrugged. "A friend of hers drove her to the bone doctor this morning. He's in New Jersey, so she won't be back until late this afternoon."

Taylor frowned. "I still say you're taking a chance."

"That's my decision," Mercedes insisted. "I'll lead Pixie out." She came beside the pony and took hold of her reins.

"Well, anyway, I'm glad you're here," Taylor said. "I think we're going to need all the help we can get today."

Chapter 2

Taylor was leading Prince Albert out to the ring when a large red van rumbled up the driveway, a billowing cloud of dust following it. Taylor tightened her grip on Prince Albert's lead line. She didn't want to risk losing her hold on him if he spooked at the noise and flying dirt.

The County HORSE van parked in front of the main building, which housed the office, tack room, and six parallel indoor box stalls, as well as more stalls against its outside wall. It was the center of all activity at Wildwood.

The van's door opened, and three official-looking people climbed out, all dressed in matching blue polo shirts that had *County HORSE Staff* embroidered on them. A balding man with the name *Frank* on his shirt looked familiar to Taylor, but she wasn't sure from where. He was followed by a woman named Angie with dark curls and large brown eyes. Last to hop down was a good-looking young man who didn't appear to be much older than Daphne. His polo embroidery read *Jon*.

They turned back to assist the four therapeutic students who followed behind, just as Mrs. LeFleur came out of the main building. She was dressed in a barn jacket and jeans, her usual ranch attire. "Hello, everyone," she greeted them warmly. "Welcome to Wildwood Stables."

A whirring noise came from the van as a back door opened and a wheelchair lift carried down a blond boy of about ten. Taylor glanced nervously at Mrs. LeFleur, who was now standing next to her.

"Uh . . . Mrs. LeFleur? What're we going to do?" Taylor whispered.

"About what?" Mrs. LeFleur asked, turning to face Taylor. Taylor jerked her head quickly toward the boy in the wheelchair.

Mrs. LeFleur chuckled. "He'll be fine. Horse-back riding is quite helpful for people in wheelchairs. Riding a horse can stimulate muscle growth and help with balance. We'll have people walk on either side of him as he rides so that if he loses his balance, he won't fall off."

"Cool!" Taylor said, genuinely impressed.

Mrs. LeFleur turned back to the group. "If everyone would please follow me, we'll go to the tack room to fit you for helmets."

The staff, two adults, one teen girl, and the boy in the wheelchair followed Mrs. LeFleur toward the main building. The teen girl had messy reddish curls that bounced around her chin. She stopped as she passed Prince Albert and gasped, reaching out to pat the horse's soft, dark neck.

"Can I ride this one?" the girl asked in an awe-filled whisper.

Taylor smiled encouragingly. "Sure, just go get a helmet first. His name is Prince Albert, and I think you'll be great on him." Taylor turned and gave a stern look to Prince Albert and whispered, "Won't she, boy?"

The girl backed away toward the main building, eyes remaining fixed on the horse. She mouthed the words *Prince Albert* a few times before turning and walking into the main building with the rest of the group.

Once the girl was out of sight, Taylor turned to Prince Albert once again. "There, you saw who's going to be riding you. She's no bigger than I am, so you'll be fine."

The group came back out, heads now covered with helmets. Their expressions ranged from pure excitement to nervous, shy looks. The girl with the curly red hair stood holding on to Jon's polo shirt, looking anxious, and Taylor beckoned for her to come toward the mounting block.

First, Daphne helped one of the adults to mount Cody. He was a tall, very thin young man in his early twenties. Angie joined Daphne on Cody's other side. They walked from the mounting block into the ring, each with a hand on the rider's thigh, looking up and encouraging him to steer the spotted horse.

Next, Prince Albert obediently lined up in front of the mounting block. Taylor flipped the reins over his neck and coaxed the red-haired girl up the steps.

Taylor smiled, looking up at the girl, trying to

mask her true emotions. Her stomach felt like a knot of butterflies — nervous and excited all at once. Hopefully, Prince Albert would behave.

"So, what's your name?" Taylor asked the girl.

"Casey," she said shyly.

"Okay, Casey. Just slide one leg into the stirrup on this side, and then swing your other leg across and into the stirrup on the other side," Taylor instructed, pointing to the spots where Casey's legs should go.

Frank approached them, smiling and ready to help out.

Just then, Prince Albert snorted and pranced forward, out of reach of Casey. The girl shrieked and jumped backward, almost knocking Frank over.

Taylor grabbed for Prince Albert. *Oh, no. Not again. Not now!*

Prince Albert did not like men. Some man had mistreated the gelding before Taylor had taken ownership of him in an animal rescue, and now he was suspicious of every man he met.

Taylor took a firm hold of Prince Albert's reins, walking him in a circle. She glanced at Casey, who was clutching Frank, wide-eyed and clearly frightened.

Taylor took a deep breath and eyed Prince Albert warily. Through clenched teeth, she muttered, "Knock it off. Behave."

"I'm scared of him," Casey said, a tremble in her voice.

"Sorry, Casey, he can be a little spooky sometimes. But he should be okay now," Taylor said.

Casey looked up at Frank, who smiled encouragingly. "Try again," he encouraged her.

Prince Albert neighed, and Taylor didn't like the fear she heard in the sound. "Could you step back?" Taylor asked Frank. "He's nervous around you."

Frank backed up quickly. "Why would he be nervous of me? Am I that scary-looking?"

"It's not your fault," Taylor said. "It's all men."

"Oh, well, as long as it's not personal," Frank quipped. "Are you sure this horse is all right to use, not too jittery?"

Taylor nodded quickly. "Sure, I'm sure. He just gets shy around men and new people. He works great with another therapeutic rider named Dana. He should be fine."

"Really?" Frank questioned doubtfully.

Taylor suddenly remembered where she'd seen Frank before — at the Rotary Horse event. "This is the horse that won Best Therapeutic Horse," she reminded him.

"Are you kidding? Him?"

"That was Dana who was riding him."

"All right, as long as you say so," Frank agreed. "I'll keep my distance." He beckoned to Casey to join him. When she came, he laid a comforting hand on her shoulder. "You can do this," he assured her. "The horse just has to get to know you."

Taylor led Casey back to where Prince Albert stood. She made sure she had a firm grip on the reins as she let Casey stroke Prince Albert's side and speak to him. When Casey seemed ready, Taylor once more brought her to the top of the mounting block and helped the girl swing one leg over Prince Albert's broad back. As soon as Casey's leg hit the saddle, Prince Albert snorted loudly, sidestepping quickly to avoid being mounted.

Casey shrieked once more, falling backward into Taylor, who caught her. Tears streamed from her eyes as she scrambled down the mounting block.

"I don't want to ride anymore!" Casey wailed, turning her back to Prince Albert and sobbing.

Frank looked at Taylor. "I thought you said you were sure."

Taylor pulled Prince Albert's head down and gazed at him sadly. "I thought I was."

Chapter 3

"What's wrong?" Daphne asked. She had come back from the ring and was leading Mandy to the mounting block. She looked at Prince Albert, the sobbing Casey, the scowling Frank, and then to Taylor. She raised her eyebrows in an unspoken question.

Taylor nodded unhappily.

"Here, you can ride Mandy," Daphne said, offering the reins to Casey. "She really likes people. Taylor will lead you while I go deal with Prince Albert, okay?"

Taylor was thankful to Daphne for stepping in and taking over. When Casey hesitated to take the reins, Taylor took them, mouthing a thank-you to Daphne.

Daphne nodded quietly and led Prince Albert away, toward the barn.

"Don't worry. Mandy isn't like Prince Albert," Taylor assured Casey as she steered her gently toward the mounting block once more. "Prince Albert is very fussy about who rides him."

Casey's eyes went wide. "Do you mean he doesn't like me?"

"No, no! He likes you."

"Well, I don't like him, either!" Casey stated firmly, her voice climbing nearly to a shout.

"That's okay. You don't have to like him," Taylor said, trying to keep her voice steady. "But you'll like Mandy here. She's very nice."

Casey stepped closer to Mandy, studying the gentle gray speckled mare. "She *does* seem nice," the girl allowed cautiously.

After a few more minutes of persuasion, Casey finally accepted that Mandy wouldn't duck out from under her as Prince Albert had done. Once she was safely seated and smiling with pride, Taylor took Mandy's reins and walked her into the corral, where she met up with Mercedes and the other mounted riders.

Frank came into the ring and began to lead the group in a series of exercises. The riders practiced balancing, by holding their arms out as they walked their horses forward. The Wildwood and HORSE staff guided the riders through poles and over obstacles. Taylor noticed that the smiles of the riders got wider and wider as they became more confident throughout the lesson.

Taylor saw that the boy with the wheelchair looked particularly happy as he rode Cody. It was as if his quiet reserve had fallen away and he'd gained new confidence as he controlled the large-bodied Colorado Ranger gelding. The boy's eyes were bright with pride, and his shoulders were back. *It must be so much easier for him to move on Cody than in his wheelchair,* she thought. *I bet he loves that.*

Before Taylor knew it, the lesson was over, and Casey was grinning ear to ear. Taylor breathed a sigh of relief as she patted Mandy on the rump, thanking her for behaving.

As they were leaving the ring, Plum Mason came out of the main building in her tan breeches and shiny black tall boots, blonde hair tucked neatly underneath a velvet riding helmet. She led Shafir — Plum leased the sleek, chestnut Arabian mare from Wildwood.

Plum's lease agreement allowed her the right to ride Shafir whenever the horse was not being used for a lesson or trail ride. In exchange, the Masons paid a monthly fee that covered a portion of Shafir's board.

Plum and Taylor had never been friendly, even though they were both in the eighth grade at Pheasant Valley Middle School. Plum was the queen bee in her clique of exclusive friends, while Taylor didn't hang with any one particular group of kids.

The HORSE group oohed and aahed at gorgeous Shafir. Ears perked, she put her head down and sniffed at everyone she passed, seeming happy to have the attention.

Angie came over to Plum and asked if she could pet Shafir. Plum nodded, then shot a smug grin to Taylor — as if Taylor really needed to be reminded that Prince Albert had not endeared himself to anyone in the HORSE group.

"Do you compete on her?" Angie asked Plum as she stroked Shafir's shiny neck.

"Yes," said Plum primly, "we've won together a bunch of times."

Taylor stared at Plum pointedly, knowing that the girl had to be thinking of the last competition, held at the swanky Ross River Ranch on the other side of Pheasant Valley. It had been Taylor's first time competing in a jump event. Even though the event was for beginners, Taylor was proud that she'd beaten the more advanced Plum — who shouldn't even have been competing in a beginner event, in Taylor's opinion.

In her heart, Taylor knew it had been a piece of very good luck that she had been riding a well-trained and experienced horse. Monty, a beautiful white Missouri Fox Trotting gelding, had once been owned by Mercedes, and she had trained him well. That was before financial disaster had hit the Gonzalez family and Mercedes' beloved horse had to be sold.

Still, Taylor *had* won that jump event. Plus she knew it made Plum furious, and Taylor was not above enjoying that fact.

Plum looked away from Taylor and focused her attention on Angie. "I have a lot of ribbons at home," Plum told the young woman.

"Wow! So are you going to the competition at Gypsy Trails coming up? They have jumping," Angie said. "Do you jump?"

"Definitely," Plum replied with confidence.

Taylor was helping Casey dismount but could hear every word that was being said.

"I should check it out. Do you know what levels they have?" Plum asked.

"All levels. You must be up pretty high, hmm?" Angie said.

Plum feigned bashfulness. "No. I'm good, but not *that* good," she said, her voice full of mock humility. "I'll be sure to enter the beginner levels."

Taylor's head whipped over to glower at Plum, who had certainly made sure to speak the word *beginner* with exaggerated clarity, just so Taylor could hear it.

Plum waved good-bye to Angie and the HORSE crowd, like a queen making an exit, but stopped when she reached Taylor. "Oh, Taylor. Did you hear? Gypsy Trails is having a show." She spoke in the annoying singsong she used when she wanted to taunt someone.

"Yeah. I heard. A little birdie told me," Taylor said flatly as she loosened Mandy's cinch.

"Great! I guess I'll be seeing you in the *beginner* class then, when I win a blue. It's okay, you can cheer for me." Plum gave her a malicious grin.

"You're not a beginner, Plum. Why don't you let *real* beginners have a chance? It's just so you can win, isn't it?"

"It's always fun to win," she cooed.

"You don't *always* win," Taylor reminded her.

"I don't know *what* you're talking about."

Just then, a loud shout came from behind the barn, and Prince Albert came trotting out toward the group, with no rider on his back. Daphne hurried behind him, a slight limp in her jog.

The gelding stopped when he spotted the other horses and Taylor looking at him. Daphne huffed up and grabbed his reins.

"He still won't let *anyone* else ride him," Daphne wheezed.

Taylor frowned and Plum smirked again.

"On second thought, maybe you should just stay home from Gypsy Trails," Plum said. "Looks like you have your work cut out for you here." And with that last insult, she led Shafir into the ring.

"Don't worry! I'll see you there!" Taylor shouted, and then turned to Daphne. "Are you all right? Did he hurt you?"

"No, I just fell trying to get on him. He backed up really quick, and I twisted my leg in a weird way," she said, grimacing as she massaged her sore knee.

Taylor looked over at Frank, who was helping the HORSE students into the van and waving to Mrs. LeFleur. "Thanks!" he called. "We'll be back next week. And good luck with that horse. Hope he doesn't hurt anyone."

Taylor's jaw dropped. *Hurt anyone?* Prince Albert would never! But her gaze flicked back to Daphne, who was sitting and rubbing her knee, a pained expression on her face.

What if he did? What if he accidentally hurt someone? What would happen?

"That horse is a menace!" Plum shouted from the ring. "He's dangerous!"

Shut up, Plum, were the words that sat on Taylor's tongue and were about to be launched, but then Taylor's gaze fell on Mrs. LeFleur. The pinched, worried look on the ranch owner's face made Taylor swallow her angry retort. She had been warned about fighting with Plum, one of Wildwood's best customers.

Behind her thick glasses, Mrs. LeFleur's dark eyes were darting between Taylor and Prince Albert. Taylor could tell that whatever she was thinking, it wasn't good news for Prince Albert. Taylor took hold of Prince Albert's reins and turned him around toward the main building. Maybe if he wasn't directly in front of Mrs. LeFleur, she would forget about his awful performance that day.

Pixie neighed from the corral. The pony trotted toward the gate, eager to be let out so she could follow Prince Albert inside.

"No, Pixie, you have to stay," Taylor said.

The County HORSE people drove off down the dirt road, and Taylor was at least thankful that Frank had said they'd be back. If Prince Albert's behavior had cost Wildwood their biggest contract, it would be just too terrible.

From the gate, Pixie whinnied pleadingly.

Daphne clicked for Pixie to come to her, but the Shetland pony wouldn't budge. With a sigh, Daphne approached the gate.

"Are you sure you're okay?" Taylor asked. "I'm so sorry about the way Prince Albert acted."

"I'm a little sore, but I'll be all right," Daphne replied. "He really does *not* want anyone else besides Dana and you to ride him, does he?"

"If you can't get him to let you ride I don't think anyone could," Taylor said. She meant it, too. Taylor had never known anyone who was a better rider or who had a more instinctive feeling for horses than Daphne.

"Why don't you hitch Prince Albert to the fence so Pixie can see him?" Daphne suggested. "I have a lesson coming in fifteen minutes, and I could use your help with it."

Daphne turned to Mrs. LeFleur. "Would that be okay?" she checked. "The girl who's coming for the lesson likes to ride Pixie, and you know how Pixie is about having Prince Albert nearby."

Taylor appreciated the way in which Daphne was trying to smooth things over. She was a real friend.

Daring to look back in Mrs. LeFleur's direction, Taylor saw that she still looked thoughtful and worried. But Wildwood's owner nodded in agreement. "Yes, of course," she said.

Taylor pressed her tongue against the back of her

teeth and looked skyward. It was what she always did when she felt tears were threatening to spill over. It was not the time to cry, but she was so worried that Prince Albert had really, finally worn out his welcome at Wildwood Stables.

Chapter 4

Fifteen minutes later, Mrs. LeFleur headed toward her car. "I need to go into town for a short while. Can you girls handle things here?"

"Sure," Mercedes told her as she walked Cody to cool him down. "Don't worry."

Mrs. LeFleur looked to Daphne, who was the oldest.

"We'll be fine," Daphne confirmed. "I won't leave until you get back." She smiled at Taylor, and something in the kindness of her expression made the tears Taylor had thought were under control jump back into her eyes once more.

"I'll be back in a minute to help you with the lesson," Taylor said, looking up again to keep the wetness from brimming over. The last thing she wanted was for Plum to see her cry.

"Sure," Daphne agreed. "Take your time."

With quick movements, Taylor hitched Prince Albert to the fence. He sputtered and Taylor patted his flank. "It's all right. I know you don't understand," she murmured in a low tone. "It's all right."

Taylor ducked her head as she made her way into the main building. All she wanted was to get away to a safe, quiet place — to hide from the world. She entered the shady middle aisle of the main building, and it wasn't until she reached Prince Albert's stall that she let her tears fall freely, covering her face with her hands.

Why did Prince Albert have to be so difficult?

She was so scared! What if Mrs. LeFleur said he had to go? Pixie wouldn't survive without him — and neither would Taylor!

A life without Prince Albert? It would be like living without a part of her body — her very heart! The idea of it made the tears come harder. Why couldn't she get through to her horse?

The sound of footsteps made Taylor lower her hands to see who was there.

Eric Mason stood beside her, his hazel green eyes filled with questions. Eric was Plum's cousin, but they couldn't be more different. About a year older than Taylor and Plum, Eric was kind and considerate. He'd started hanging out at Wildwood since Westheimer's, another ranch nearby, had to cut staff and he'd lost his job there. Taylor was glad to have him around more.

She laughed self-consciously through her tears, embarrassed that he was seeing her in such a state. "Prince Albert is going to be thrown out of here if he doesn't start behaving," she explained.

"Did he give you a hard time with the County HORSE group?" he asked.

Taylor nodded as she wiped her eyes. "He wouldn't let the girl who was supposed to ride him mount," Taylor explained. "Prince Albert *has* to be a working horse. I can't afford to keep him otherwise."

"I know. But don't worry. He'll come around," Eric said kindly.

"Thanks, but I'm not so sure anymore," Taylor replied. "He's been here for three months. Time's running out."

"Jojo is like that," Eric said, referring to his Tennessee

walking horse gelding that he still boarded over at Westheimer's. "Jojo will only let me ride him."

"Really?" Taylor said, tilting her head with interest. "I guess that's okay, though, because no one else but you *has* to ride him. Right?"

"Not exactly," Eric said. "Remember how I wanted to talk to Mrs. LeFleur about working here?"

Taylor nodded. When Eric was on Westheimer's staff he'd been allowed to board Jojo there for free. Now that he didn't work there anymore, he would have to pay. So he had asked Mrs. LeFleur for a job.

"Well, she can't hire anyone right now. She reminded me that Daphne, Mercedes, and you all volunteer," Eric said.

"And Travis, too," Taylor added. Her best friend, Travis Ryan, repaired things around Wildwood so Taylor and he could hang out.

"Yeah, and Travis," Eric agreed. "The point is that she can't pay anyone, but she did say I could board Jojo here for half price — if I agreed to work a little and to feed him myself."

"That's great!" Taylor said. It meant Eric would be around all the time.

Taylor liked Eric a lot, and she suspected that he liked her in the same way; suspected, but was not completely sure. He came over and talked to her all the time, and he really seemed to care what happened to her, like now.

"Daphne said that if she could use Jojo for lessons sometimes, she'd groom him and exercise him when I wasn't around," Eric added. "So, I have to get him to take on other riders. Maybe we could work on it together when I'm here."

"Sure, I'd like that!" Taylor agreed. "When should we start?"

"Ralph is lending me his trailer on Wednesday to bring Jojo over here. I have soccer practice after school on Monday and Tuesday. So does Wednesday sound okay?"

"Wednesday I start my free riding lessons over at Ross River Ranch," Taylor told him.

"I remember — the ones you won in the last competition," Eric recalled.

Taylor nodded. "I'm so excited," she admitted. "I have to get really good, really fast. I want to enter a jumping event coming up at Gypsy Trails. Actually, I kind of have to enter, since I pretty much challenged Plum just now."

"Why did you do that?" Eric asked with an uneasy grimace.

"You know how Plum can be," Taylor replied.

Eric laughed grimly. "Nobody knows how annoying my cousin can be more than I do," he said. "Still . . . you challenged her? Why?"

"She just makes so mad."

"Don't let her get to you."

Taylor knew it was sensible advice, and she'd heard — and tried — it before. Why *did* Plum bother her so much? It had always been that way. Plum was arrogant and rich and always made a point of looking down on Taylor and everyone else. "I don't know. She's just so . . . mean."

Eric nodded thoughtfully. "She *can* be mean sometimes, I guess."

Taylor rolled her eyes, but she decided to drop the subject. Plum *was* Eric's cousin, after all, and he probably felt he had to stick up for her, at least a little.

"How's Spots doing?" Taylor asked, to change the subject.

Spots was the young fawn they'd rescued from the woods. Normally, they wouldn't have touched a young animal sitting in underbrush, as Spots had been. Most likely the mother deer was going to return for it. But, after seeing a dead doe on the side of the road, Taylor had checked on the little fawn a while later. It was clear that the fawn had been there alone a long time. It had been making a heartrending, pitiful sound, bleating like a goat, crying for its mother to feed it.

Eric and Taylor walked up the aisle toward the front entrance of the main building. Spots's new home was in the tack room, near the front door.

Before looking in on Spots, Taylor stepped out front to check if Daphne's riding lesson had arrived. There was still no sign of the student. Daphne and Mercedes were sitting on the split-rail fence of the front corral. Pixie and Prince Albert grazed peacefully on either side of the gate, content just to be together, while Mandy and Cody also munched on the taller grass that grew beside another fence post. With a wave to her friends, Taylor ducked back into the main building and joined Eric in the tack room.

Spots sat in the far corner, sleeping soundly, his spindly legs tucked under his delicate body. His reddish coat was dotted with the white spots for which he'd been named.

"I talked to the vet, Dr. Somers, last week," Eric told Taylor. "She thinks Spots is at least four months old."

"How can she tell?" Taylor asked.

"She said that the last deer births of the season are usually around the end of June. We found Spots in early November, which would make him about four months old, and Dr. Somers figures, because he's still so small and still has his spots, he's probably not any older than five months, at the most. But because of his small size, she thinks he's closer to four months," he said. "I looked it up online, and a deer usually molts and loses its spots by seven months."

Taylor was impressed. Eric always knew so much about everything. He went to a prestigious private school on an academic scholarship. His brains made him that much more appealing, in Taylor's opinion.

"I just fed him, so he should be falling asleep soon," Eric added.

"Is that why you're here today, to take care of Spots?" Taylor asked.

"Since I don't have an after-school job anymore, I have time. And I like the little guy," he said. "Now I'm just waiting for my aunt Beverly to come get Plum so I can catch a ride with them."

Taylor groaned — a little louder than she meant to. A few weeks ago, Beverly Mason had driven so fast down Wildwood Lane that she had spooked Prince Albert. Taylor had been walking him on a lead line when Prince Albert reared and broke free, running out onto the steep and winding main road. Mercedes' mother had been driving around the corner, and she crashed into a tree to avoid hitting the gelding.

And that was the reason Mercedes had been forbidden to come to Wildwood anymore. Her mother had decided that the conditions at the ranch weren't safe.

Eric sighed. Along with Travis, he had helped Taylor search for her runaway horse on that awful day. "Oh, yeah," he said. "I know you're not a fan of Aunt Beverly."

"Sorry, but no," Taylor replied.

"She does drive too fast, sometimes," Eric conceded.

And she wouldn't take any responsibility for what she did, Taylor recalled indignantly. But again, she decided not to say anything to embarrass Eric about his family. He couldn't help who his relatives were.

"Don't worry," Eric said again. "We'll find a time to work with Jojo and Prince Albert. We'll get them straightened out."

It was going to be so great working with Eric. He was smart with horses. If anyone could make this work, he could.

Or maybe not . . .

"Wait a minute," Taylor said as a worrisome thought suddenly hit her. "You're not the best person to try to ride Prince Albert."

Eric looked puzzled — and a little hurt. "Why not?"

"You're a guy."

"Yeah . . . so?"

"Remember how Prince Albert acted the first time he saw you?" Taylor reminded him. Prince Albert had bucked and neighed, causing Eric to jump back, so startled he nearly fell to the ground. "He doesn't like guys."

"I remember — but he's used to me by now, don't you think?" Eric replied. "I'm standing right here, and he's not freaking out. Maybe he's over the whole guy thing. He's been here a while now."

Taylor hoped he was right, but she wasn't so sure. Prince Albert never seemed to forget anything.

"He's calmer now, it's true," Taylor admitted. "But after this morning with Casey and Daphne . . . I just don't want you to get hurt."

"He'll be okay," Eric assured her as he patted Prince Albert's flank.

Prince Albert whinnied, and Taylor didn't like the sound of it. She thought she heard something nervous and high-strung in his tone.

Taylor heard a car pull in and knew it must be Daphne's next riding lesson. "I'd better go," she said despite the fact that she didn't want to leave Eric. "Daphne wants me to help with her lesson."

"Okay," Eric agreed. "Would it be all right if I called you later tonight?"

Taylor's heart seemed to skip a beat.

"Sure," she said.

It was the first good news she'd had all day.

Chapter 5

When Taylor got home early that evening, her mother, Jennifer Henry, was still dressed in the white shirt and black pants she always wore to her job at the Pheasant Valley Diner. Taylor's parents had divorced back in the spring. Jennifer had started her own catering business, and it was beginning to do well, but not so well that Jennifer could quit her job at the diner.

"You're just in time," Jennifer told Taylor. "Claire is here to help me with a birthday party I'm catering tomorrow. But we could really use your help. I have about a zillion cupcakes to frost before I can go to sleep tonight."

Taylor rolled her eyes and slumped. Icing cupcakes was not what she was in the mood to do after the long day she'd had. But she would be happy to see Claire Black, her mother's best friend since childhood. Claire was an animal rehabilitator, which meant she rescued injured animals of all kinds. Ever since she was small, Taylor had gone with Claire on her rescue missions. It was on one of these rescues that Claire and Taylor had come upon Prince Albert and Pixie locked and abandoned in a barn.

"Hey, Taylor," Claire said when Taylor followed her mother into the kitchen. Claire sat at the kitchen table with a half-iced cupcake in her hand, finishing the other side. Bunny, Claire's brindle-coated pit bull, came out from under the table to greet Taylor by licking her hand.

"Hi, Claire. Hey, Bunny." Taylor rubbed Bunny's head as she spoke.

"How are things down at Wildwood?" Claire asked.

"Wildwood is fine, it's Prince Albert who's driving me crazy," Taylor said as she sat at the table and picked up an unfrosted cupcake.

Jennifer plucked it from Taylor's fingers. "Go wash your hands. I'm nuking you some meat loaf, mashed potatoes, and peas I brought from the diner."

"Why is sweet Prince Albert making you nuts?" Claire inquired as Taylor moved to the sink to wash up.

"He was so difficult this morning," Taylor said, and went on to tell her mother and Claire about the frustrating struggle to get her horse to cooperate.

Claire shook her head sympathetically. "Poor guy."

"Poor guy?!" Taylor exploded, returning to her seat at the table. "What about poor me? I'm the one who has to get him to behave. Mrs. LeFleur needs him to work for his room and board."

Jennifer put Taylor's dinner down in front of her. "That's how I feel when I ask you to help out around here. After you help me with this I want you to clean your room. It's a mess."

"Oh, Mom, I'm so tired," Taylor complained.

"So am I," Jennifer countered.

"Don't bicker, you two. We'll get these cupcakes iced and call it a night," Claire suggested.

"You're right," Jennifer agreed.

Taylor ate her meal and then, after washing her hands and putting her dish in the dishwasher, got an icing spreader and began topping the small cakes with frosty white icing. She had finished fifteen cupcakes when her cell phone rang.

For a second, Taylor thought it might be Eric. But

from the ring tone, she knew it was Travis. She'd made Travis's special ring tone the theme song from the Batman movies because Travis was a devoted comic book lover.

Wiping her sticky fingers on a dish towel, she plucked the phone from the pocket of her jeans. "Hi. How are you feeling?" Travis had been home all week with a stomach bug.

"Still horrible," Travis mumbled. "Really, really horrible."

As Travis spoke, Taylor could picture his round face, topped by a blond buzz cut, looking pale and unhappy. "We miss you down at the barn." Travis wasn't a rider, but he liked to come down so he and Taylor could continue to spend as much time together as they always had. Mrs. LeFleur was always happy to see him since he was talented at fixing all sorts of things.

"I'll be back in a minute," Taylor said to her mom and Claire, rising from the table.

"One minute," Jennifer said.

"Okay." Taylor wandered into the living room and spread out on the couch. Travis filled her in on his illness and how awful he felt. But then a beep broke through their conversation and her caller ID read ERIC MASON.

"I'm getting another call," Taylor said. "Can I call you back?"

"It's that Eric guy, isn't it?" Travis said with an edge of annoyance. Even though she and Travis had always been buddies, Travis seemed jealous of Eric.

"Why do you think it's Eric?" Taylor asked.

"If it was anyone else you'd keep talking to me," Travis judged correctly.

Taylor was eager to take Eric's call before she lost it. "Yeah, well, I'll call you back. Bye."

"Bye," Travis grumbled.

Taylor quickly clicked into Eric's call. "Hello? Hello, Eric?"

But Eric was already gone. Taylor was just about to call him back when Jennifer shouted from the kitchen. "Taylor, I heard you say bye. What are you doing now?"

"I just have to call somebody now," Taylor replied. "Please. It's very important."

"What's so important?"

Taylor had to think about that. It seemed very, very important to her, but her mother wouldn't see it that way. "It will just be a short call," she said, trying a new approach.

"No way!" Jennifer shouted. "No more phone tonight."

"Mom," Taylor wailed. "Please. Two minutes."

"No! Come in and help!"

"The cupcakes are calling," Claire sang out in a jollier tone.

Her shoulders drooping, Taylor got off the couch and slouched back to the kitchen. First, Prince Albert acted so badly. Now her mother wasn't cooperating, and she'd missed Eric's call. Taylor would be glad when this day was over. It had been completely rotten, and it didn't seem to be getting any better.

On Wednesday afternoon, Taylor chewed on her thumb nervously as she walked across a field, up to the large white barn at Ross River Ranch. Today she would have her first lesson at the fancy stables, and she was feeling a little intimidated already. She had dressed in her nicest pair of breeches (which had only a few stains on them), her worn but functional tall boots (which had once belonged to Daphne), and her Pheasant Valley softball sweatshirt (which was her only clean one. She'd been too busy these days to do much laundry).

Taylor reached the barn's large sliding door, which was open just enough to walk through. The aisle was wide, with soft lights and fans hanging from the ceiling. Taylor was amazed every time she entered the barn at its immaculate cleanliness and polished appearance. Most barns had a sort of dusty smell of hay mixed with the sweat of horses, but this barn had little scent at all. All the stalls displayed shiny gold nameplates and a bar from which hung horse blankets embroidered with each owner's initials.

From the other end of the aisle, she heard the telltale *clip-clop* of hooves on the smooth cement as a familiar white gelding walked in. It was Monty, the Missouri Fox Trotting Horse that had once belonged to Mercedes. Taylor took out her cell phone to text her friend: THINK I'M RIDING MONTY. COME VISIT!

Before Mercedes' family moved to Pheasant Valley, they had been hit with money troubles and sold all their horses to a man who owned another barn in Connecticut. That man had given Monty to his niece, who lived near

Pheasant Valley. Mercedes later learned that the niece had sold Monty, along with a few other horses, to Ross River Ranch. She was happy to hear that Monty was nearby, but Mercedes couldn't just visit the exclusive ranch without a reason.

A neatly dressed man in a white polo shirt embroidered with the Ross River logo and polished paddock boots held on to Monty's lead line. He looked to be in his forties, but he was only a little taller than Taylor.

"Taylor Henry?" he asked. He had a slight Spanish accent and a friendly, weathered face.

Taylor nodded slowly, surprised that he knew her name. "Yeah. Um, hi," she replied.

"I'm Enrique, the head groom here. I was told you'd be coming. Pleased to meet you." He extended a rough, leathery hand to shake. His firm grip was slightly crushing, and Taylor noticed that he smelled of soap and hay. He smiled at her once more, clipped Monty to the cross ties, and walked into a room down the aisle, on the left.

A moment later Enrique returned, holding a light brown saddle with a fuzzy girth attached, a black saddle pad that displayed the Ross River insignia in white, and a bridle slung across his shoulder.

Taylor held out her hands, ready to begin tacking up Monty. But Enrique only stopped, gave her a quizzical look, and then stepped to her left. He tossed the saddle pad onto Monty's back.

Taylor dropped her outstretched hands and turned to watch. Enrique glanced at her out of the corner of his eye and chuckled.

"New here, hmm?" he asked with a grin.

Taylor blushed, embarrassed to be so obvious. "Could you tell? Really, it's okay, you don't have to tack him up. I've got it, thank you," she babbled. She knew that fancy barns often had grooms who got the horses ready for their riders, but she had never expected to be on the receiving end of this luxury.

"Can't let you. It's my job," Enrique said, tightening the girth. Monty's ears swiveled as he turned to give a little nip in protest to the girth's increased pressure. Enrique bopped him lightly on the nose with his free hand, and Monty snapped straight and stared forward, looking like a pouting child.

Grabbing the bridle, Enrique fit it on Monty's head, wiggling the bit into his mouth. Monty tongued at the bit, seeming to ponder the new item. Enrique pulled

Monty's forelock out from under the brow band and handed the reins to Taylor.

"Here you go. Mr. Hobbes will meet you outside in the main ring. You can go warm up in the meantime," Enrique said with a nod toward the large ring she had competed in not too long ago. He patted Monty on the rump as he left, with a wave to Taylor over his shoulder.

Taylor stood there, holding the reins, still a little nervous about her approaching lesson and meeting Keith Hobbes. She turned to Monty, who looked back at her expectantly, as if to say *Well? Are we going to stand here all day?* Taylor took a deep breath and headed out toward the ring.

It was a clear day, great for riding. Not too hot, not too cold. Taylor brought Monty into the center of the ring and adjusted the stirrups. She noticed the logo on the saddle. She recognized it from the horse catalogs she loved to peruse, just for the fun of it: Hermès. *This is the most expensive saddle I've ever sat on*, she realized, and a small shiver of excitement ran through her. What a different world this was!

She checked the girth before mounting and then lifted one leg into the stirrup closest to her, hoisting her body up while swinging her right leg over. She squared herself, making sure that she was properly balanced before clucking Monty into a walk.

As they made their way around the ring, Taylor tried to relax her abdomen and feel her hips sway back and forth with the rhythm of Monty's gate. When Mercedes had been teaching her English-style riding, she'd told Taylor that it was important to stay relaxed and supple; a tense rider couldn't accomplish anything.

Taylor let the rhythm of Monty's steady movement lull her into a daydream. She imagined herself riding in an Olympic stadium jumping competition, dressed in tan Tailored Sportsman breeches and a white high-collared shirt, her navy hunt coat fitting her form. She lifted her chin as she imagined the words *Now entering the ring, Taylor Henry riding Montana Wind Dancer* booming forth from the stadium's speakers, the imagined announcer's British accent echoing around the arena.

With her imagination still going strong, she made a kissing sound that moved Monty into a trot. She was rising up and down as Mercedes had taught her, following the rhythm of Monty's legs, imagining the spectators for the Olympic event admiring her poise and confidence.

"Diagonals!" shouted a voice, and Taylor was so startled she slid to the left, and kept sliding. . . .

Chapter 6

Taylor quickly recovered her seat and looked over to where the voice had come from. A short and skinny man in a dark blue baseball cap that read USEF stood at the entrance to the ring. White tufts of hair were visible from under his cap, and his thick, gray eyebrows were raised as he watched Taylor ride. He wore a simple black T-shirt, customary tan breeches, and polished black tall boots.

This must be the famous Keith Hobbes — a retired United States Equestrian Federation judge, an A circuit competitor, and a former Olympic dressage team trainer. Taylor had looked him up online when she'd won the Ross River lessons, and she was more than a little nervous to meet such a distinguished rider.

And of course he'd have to notice her diagonals first! This part of English riding gave Taylor more trouble than anything else. It was so difficult to tell which of the horse's front legs was swinging forward without looking! She brought Monty down to a walk and moved toward Keith, suddenly much tenser than she was before. "Hi, my name is Taylor," she said when she was close to him. "Are you my instructor?"

"Keith Hobbes," he responded, touching the brim of his cap in greeting. "Now, go pick up the correct diagonal. Do a warm-up lap."

Taylor obeyed, guiding Monty over to the rail. She glanced down to Monty's outside leg, rising up out of the saddle as it came forward.

Wow, he doesn't waste any time, Taylor thought as she tried to keep the up-down rhythm.

"Close your hip angle," Keith called out. Taylor was glad that he didn't seem as annoyed and hurried as Mercedes often did. "You're a Western rider, aren't you?" he observed.

"Does it still show?" she asked, chagrined. Taylor wanted to believe that she was moving back and forth between the two styles with grace. She had first learned

Western style at Westheimer's Ranch when she was around eight, but now that she wanted to jump, she had to learn English. There was no jumping in Western riding.

"Yep. It shows a little," he replied. Taylor bent forward at her hip, trying to mask her Western riding background as best she could. Since Western riders generally learned to "sit on their back pockets," she had to relearn and practice being more perched in the saddle.

"We're going to work on your form a bit today. Okay?" Keith's voice rang through the ring, calm and instructional. "Now, I want you to bring your lower leg back and push more weight into your heels," he said.

Taylor tried to do both, all the while keeping the posting trot.

"Good. Much better!" Keith praised her.

Taylor smiled at his encouraging words. Mercedes almost never gave her any positive reinforcement. Mercedes wasn't mean, and Taylor was grateful for the instruction she was giving her, but the girl had a bossy, critical streak that could be hard to take. It was just nice to hear a compliment for a change.

"I want to see more bend in your arm. Now, ask for a canter," Keith instructed as Taylor sat down and nudged

Monty into the quicker, three-beat gate. "Check your lead! Is it correct?"

She broke Monty back into the trot. "I guess not? Uh . . . sorry . . . but what's a lead?" Taylor asked, feeling uninformed and embarrassed. He probably expected his rider would know these things already. Had she disappointed him on their very first lesson?

Keith strode toward Taylor, who awaited a verbal smack much like Mercedes would have given her, making her feel dumber than she already did.

"A correct lead is when your horse's inside leg stretches out more than his outside. You'll feel your inside hip drop more than your outside, and that's how you'll know," he explained calmly without a hint of annoyance. "Also, while you're still learning, you can glance down and check. It's really only in the show ring that you don't want a judge to see you do that." He smiled and turned back to his spot in the center of the ring. "Believe me, I'd know."

They continued with their lesson, moving on into two-point, over ground poles, and then practicing with small cross rails. Taylor began to relax, now knowing that Keith wouldn't make fun of her or be disappointed by her inexperience. He praised her when she did something right and corrected her with simple instructions and tips when she did something wrong. Taylor was just bringing Monty over a low vertical when she noticed Mercedes leaning on the rail, watching them.

"Keep practicing," Keith said. "I'll be back in a minute."

"Okay," Taylor agreed as she smiled at Mercedes and waved.

Mercedes lifted her chin in response, never taking her sight off Monty, her eyes burning into the horse. It was as if she was remembering a different time, when Monty was her horse, and hers alone.

Taylor was so distracted by the distant and sad look on Mercedes' face that, after landing her low jump, she didn't properly guide Monty to the center of the ring. Sensing Taylor's inattention, Monty made a beeline for Mercedes.

Taylor pulled on Monty's left rein and pushed her right leg into his side to correct his direction, but Monty insisted on trotting up to the fence, sticking his nose through the rails, and nudging Mercedes. Taylor was impressed by Monty's loyalty to Mercedes. He had never forgotten her.

A smile broke through the gloom of Mercedes' face as the horse nuzzled her, and she stretched forward to stroke his soft nose. With her free hand Mercedes reached into her back pocket and produced a sugar cube. Monty extended his neck to lick up the small, sweet block.

Taylor was always surprised to see this soft side of Mercedes. The only other time she'd witnessed it was back at the horse show when Mercedes had seen Monty again after so long. "Montana Wind Dancer," Mercedes crooned. "How are you, Monty?"

The horse sniffed Mercedes, his ears forward attentively.

Mercedes stroked his white mane. "Don't worry, boy. I'll find a way to get you back," she said. "I have no idea how, but I'll figure out something. There's got to be a way to do it."

At the other end of the ring, Keith returned with a tall blonde whom Taylor recognized immediately.

"What's Plum's mother doing here?" Taylor hissed to Mercedes.

Without turning much, Mercedes cut her eyes over to Beverly Mason.

Taylor kept her head down, not wanting to make it obvious that they were studying the adults. A burst of laughter traveled across the ring as Keith Hobbes and Beverly Mason shared a joke. "They seem to know each other," Taylor observed.

Once again Mercedes shrugged, rolling her eyes. "It happens. The horse people in an area tend to know one another. When we lived in Connecticut we knew everyone around us who had horse farms."

Why was Keith talking to Plum's mother? Taylor realized that in just this short time, she had come to feel possessive of him. Keith was *her* teacher. She didn't want to share him with Plum. Was that why Beverly Mason was here, to book a lesson?

"I don't like the way they seem to be talking about Monty," Mercedes commented.

Taylor tucked in her chin and cast another furtive glance across the ring. Keith was pointing toward Monty as he said something that caused the woman to nod in agreement.

Chapter 7

Taylor's skin bristled with excitement in the crisp afternoon air as she pulled the halter on over Prince Albert's ears. She couldn't tell if it was because of the chilly breeze or because today was the day Eric would trailer Jojo over so they could work on getting the horses to accept other riders.

"You'll be okay with Eric, won't you?" Taylor urged her horse. "I know you don't like guys, but he's really very nice."

Taylor knew he would respond to the sound of her voice, as he always did. For fun, she added a question. "So, do you think you could cooperate and let him ride you? At the very least, don't try to scare him out of his wits. Can you do that?"

Prince Albert whinnied, tossing his black mane.

Was it a yes or a no? Did it mean anything at all?

Taylor hoped it was a yes and decided to stay positive. "Okay, I'm assuming you're saying you will. Good boy."

She brought Prince Albert into the main aisle, clipping him to cross ties. Looking around, she noted the distinct difference between the smells and sights of Ross River Ranch and Wildwood Stables. Although they were neat here at Wildwood, it was not nearly as immaculate as the elite Ross River. She glanced around at the stall doors and chewed her lip thoughtfully as she envisioned what it would look like if the old, dusty stalls had shiny gold plaques and blanket racks in front of every door.

Taylor patted Prince Albert's neck as she walked past him and into the tack room. She stooped to grab her grooming tote from the corner. It consisted of two used curry combs that Mercedes had given her and one she'd found on the floor in the tack room, used hard and soft brushes Mrs. LeFleur had given her, a mane brush Dana's mother had presented her as a gift, and an old hoof pick she had found in one of the paddocks. The only items Taylor had purchased with her own money were a bottle of fly spray and some spray-on coat conditioner.

As she walked back into the aisle she saw the rusty old Westheimer Ranch truck rumble down the drive towing a silver horse trailer, a thick plume of dust following close behind it. Prince Albert nickered in response to the loud truck, and Taylor quickly tried to look as busy as possible as she fought back a grin of excitement. Somehow that smile came to her face every time Eric was around.

Grabbing a curry comb, she brushed Albert's coat in small circles, removing the dirt and grass Albert had rolled in. She shook the curry comb to remove the excess hair, but paused and looked at it. No hair had stuck to the comb as it often did. Taylor had been so busy that she'd barely had time to recognize that the weather was turning colder. Glancing down at her fly spray, she realized that there was now no need for it. The coming of colder weather meant no more insects.

Prince Albert sputtered once again, seeming to welcome the arrival of the new horse. Taylor straightened her shirt, smoothed down her hair, and put her curry comb back in the tote. Leaving Prince Albert's side, she took a deep breath and walked toward the horse trailer.

A young man in overalls pulled the truck and trailer to a stop in front of the main building. Eric sat beside him in the passenger seat.

"Hey, Taylor," Rick, the ranch hand at Westheimer's, greeted her as he climbed out of the truck. "Is Mrs. LeFleur around?"

"In the office," Taylor replied. "What's up?"

"Nothing much. Ralph wants me to ask her if she'd like to split another load of hay. Saves money, buying lots of bales all at once."

Taylor jerked her thumb over her shoulder. "She's right inside." Looking back to the cab of the truck, she saw that Eric had already slipped out and gone around to open the rear doors. She heard the familiar sound of hooves clanging on the steel unloading ramp.

"Hey! Need any help unloading?" she called, hurrying around to join him.

Eric turned to her. "I think we're all set," he said with a smile as he coaxed his black Tennessee walking horse down the ramp. Taylor took a minute to admire its straight profile, muscular arched neck, and high-set tail.

Eric spoke to the gelding in a low, calm voice. "Easy, boy. There ya go, almost done. . . ." The way Eric spoke to Jojo made Taylor feel a little less silly for all the talking she did to Prince Albert.

Jojo finished backing and stood in front of them, looking around and taking in his surroundings. His ears swiveled like radars and his nostrils flared, full of the scent of the unfamiliar barn.

"Let's get this started then," Taylor suggested. "I just need to tack up Prince Albert, and we'll be good to go."

Eric nodded, following Taylor into the barn, Jojo in tow. He clipped Jojo to the cross ties behind Prince Albert. "Would you mind if I borrowed your grooming stuff? I left mine back at Westheimer's."

Taylor glanced dubiously down at her ragtag grooming items. "They're sort of . . . worn," she said, embarrassed.

"Do they work?"

"Well, yes, but . . ."

"Then there's no problem," Eric concluded firmly. He grinned and held out his hand. Smiling back, and suddenly feeling more comfortable, Taylor handed over the bag.

"Well, guess you won't be needing this," Eric said,

nodding to the fly spray. "Good thing about it getting cold — no more bugs."

"Funny, you read my mind. I was just thinking that. Since it's getting colder, do you think I should try to find blankets for Prince Albert and Pixie?"

"Yeah, it gets pretty chilly at night now. I mean, they should be fine for the time being, but when the winter really hits they're each going to need a thick blanket. This place isn't heated like Ross River Ranch, after all." Eric knelt and picked out Jojo's hooves. Jojo lifted each leg gingerly as Eric scraped out the debris inside.

Taylor chewed her lip, brows furrowed. "How much does a good blanket cost, do you think?"

"Around a hundred and fifty, I'd say. There are always fancier blankets that cost more, but the average for a sturdy turnout blanket would probably be about that."

He stood and ran his hand along Jojo's sleek coat. "I'll be right back," he said, and hurried away down the aisle. He soon returned with a saddle and bridle. "A blanket for Pixie would cost less, of course," he resumed their conversation as he tossed the saddle onto Jojo's back. "Ya know, being smaller — less material and all."

Taylor nodded, not happy to have heard the figures. That was three hundred dollars she didn't have — even if Pixie's blanket cost a little less. She didn't want them to be cold, but how would she afford everything?

Eric looked across Jojo's back at her. "What's the matter?"

"Horse stuff can get so expensive. I wish all of it was cheaper. It would sure make my life easier," she admitted.

Eric chuckled, tightening the cinch. Jojo gritted his teeth in protest but made no move against it. "It sure would," Eric agreed. "It stinks sometimes, doesn't it? Back when I worked over at Westheimer's most of the money I made went right back out to pay for Jojo's stuff. Now that I've been laid off I don't know what I'm going to do."

"If only we had money like the people at Ross River," Taylor said. "The wealth is intense over there. They don't even groom and tack up their own horses!" Taylor slid the snaffle bit into Prince Albert's mouth. After that, she reached up and worked his ears under the bridle's crown piece. "I kind of like this part of riding, though. It helps you bond with your horse."

Eric nodded, taking a hold of Jojo's reins. "I agree. So I guess you're lucky that you're not super rich like them. You get more out of it, since you put more work into it."

Taylor paused and nodded thoughtfully. She had never really looked at her struggles as positive things, only as necessary chores. Sometimes she even felt sorry for herself, wishing things came easier, and that she, Prince Albert, and Pixie didn't have to constantly worry about earning their keep.

But what Eric said made sense, in a way. The closeness she felt to Prince Albert and Pixie was also a product of the fact that the three of them worked together as a sort of team.

"You're right," she admitted. "Still, not having money doesn't exactly feel lucky."

"I know what you mean," Eric agreed. "I might have some luck coming up, though."

"Really?"

"A guy I know just got a job in the horse section of a big pet supply chain, and he says they throw tons of stuff away when it's just a little outdated. He offered to sell me some of it at a big discount, and I could give some of it to you."

Taylor's jaw dropped. This was too good to be true. "Are you sure?" she asked.

Eric nodded. "Yeah. Why not? And since he's getting the things for free I don't think he'll sell it to me for much. I hope not, anyway."

"I'd pay you for it, of course," Taylor added. This was great news. Whatever she'd have to pay would be less than if she went to the store for the supplies. She had a little money left from her birthday last spring. Her mother might give her some, and she could also ask her father.

"Let's see how much he wants for the stuff first," Eric suggested. "Maybe we can split the cost of things like shampoo and horse treats."

"That would be awesome," Taylor agreed. Eric was so great. She liked him more each time they were together.

"C'mon. You ready?" Eric asked.

Taylor took hold of Prince Albert's reins and nodded. "Ready as I'll ever be." She turned to Prince Albert and asked, "You're going to behave for Eric, aren't you?" Although she knew that Eric was a very experienced rider, Taylor had her doubts about how Prince Albert would react. She knew that there was only so much even the best rider could do with a thousand-pound animal that simply didn't want to be ridden.

And there was the other problem, too.

Despite her little talk with Prince Albert, she was pretty sure he still did not like men . . . not even young, wonderful ones like Eric.

Chapter 8

They walked out of the stable into the main ring, Taylor latching the gate behind them. Eric looked up from checking and retightening Jojo's cinch to say, "Almost forgot. Helmets. Don't want to try to ride a new horse without one."

Taylor thumped herself in the forehead, amazed that she could have forgotten. "You're right! Hold Prince Albert for a second while I run in and grab them, please?" she said, handing the reins over to Eric's outstretched hand. She jogged back into the tack room, snatching a helmet for Eric off of its hanging spot on the wall. Next, Taylor grabbed her own helmet from her tack box and then jogged back out to the ring.

Eric stood there, looking completely relaxed in the afternoon light, a horse in each hand. Taylor handed him a helmet. "Here, this should fit you."

"Thanks," Eric said, letting go of the horses as he placed the helmet on his head and clipped the buckle. He bobbed his head around to make sure it was a secure fit. "Perfect."

"Horse swap time," Taylor said once her helmet was on. She held out Prince Albert's reins so Eric could take over.

Taylor took Jojo's reins and led him over to the mounting block. Eric stayed where he was, stroking Prince Albert's neck. Taylor couldn't make out what Eric was saying, but she was sure he was trying to reassure Prince Albert that he would be a good rider, if Prince Albert would let him.

Jojo danced around as Taylor stuck one foot in the stirrup and swung herself gently onto Jojo's back. "Nice boy," she praised him. *So far, so good*, she thought.

She pushed her heels into Jojo's sides and clucked for a walk. Jojo didn't move. Taylor asked again, clucking louder and kicking a bit harder.

Still nothing.

"Try telling him to 'walk on.' He's trained for voice cues, so that might work. I told you he was weird with other riders," Eric called out from the other side of the ring as he approached the mounting block.

"Walk on," Taylor said in a firm voice.

She waited a moment but was suddenly lurched backward in the saddle as Jojo set off at a run. "Whoa! Walk! Walk! Not gallop!" she shouted to Jojo.

The horse ignored her frantic commands.

With her free hand, Taylor grabbed the saddle horn for added support and pulled back on the reins with her other hand. "Whoa! Slow down! Stop!" she shouted as she raced around the ring at a terrifying speed. Taylor and Jojo barreled around the ring for a full lap, and Jojo was clearly heading for another.

Eric climbed on top of the mounting block and cupped his hands around his mouth for a megaphone effect. "Jojo, hooooo!" he called out in a deep voice, holding the "o" in a bass note. Jojo slid to a stop in front of the mounting block, almost unseating Taylor completely.

Prince Albert glanced over, not seeming phased by the excitement.

Taylor panted and straightened herself, still clutching the horn with white knuckles. She looked up at Eric, her helmet askew, brown hair poking out of the sides. "Thanks," she gulped, trying to catch her breath.

"You all right?" Eric asked, climbing down from the mounting block.

Although she was extremely shaken, she nodded. "Yeah, I'm fine." She took a deep breath. "Whew! Jojo sure has some speed." Taylor unclenched her hand from the horn and flexed it, regaining feeling.

Eric chuckled and patted Jojo's neck before turning and walking back to the mounting block. "Yeah, he likes to run. We barrel race, so he's used to going from zero to sixty very fast. Sorry, I should have warned you he might do that." Eric patted Jojo on the neck. "Good staying on there, though, cowgirl."

Although Taylor's heart had finally calmed down, it sped right back up again with the compliment. She was glad that her face was already flushed from the excitement so he couldn't tell she was blushing.

Without being asked, Jojo began to walk around the outside of the ring at a slow pace, seeming to realize they weren't in a barrel-racing pattern after all. Taylor clutched the reins, prepared for another takeoff. None came, though, and as they rounded the edges of the arena, Jojo's head hung low and relaxed.

"Hey, I think he's starting to like —" Taylor was cut off. She had looked up just in time to see Eric swing his other leg over Price Albert's back and into the saddle.

At first, Taylor was surprised that Eric was actually riding Prince Albert. Her surprise quickly turned into fear as Prince Albert began the most vigorous bucking she had ever seen.

Eric gripped the reins in one hand. Taylor knew he was trying to keep Prince Albert's head up, which would prevent him from bucking. Eric's other hand remained outstretched for balance, a lot like she had seen in bronco busting competitions on TV.

Taylor stared wide-eyed and mouth agape as Eric was tossed forward and back. Prince Albert was in midair when his saddle slipped off to the side, sending Eric somer-saulting through the air.

With a painful-sounding thud, Eric hit the ground. He bounced nearly a foot before sliding in the dirt. In the next second, when Prince Albert completed his buck, his hooves were only inches from Eric's head.

Taylor gasped and quickly dismounted, her heart in her throat. Prince Albert, now spooked by the sideways saddle, galloped around the ring, flinging his body up in the air. Taylor's eyes darted from Eric's still figure on the ground, to the panicked horse bolting around the ring, to Jojo's reins in her hand. Her mind raced. What should she do?

It took a moment to slow her speeding thoughts. First she would have to get Prince Albert so he wouldn't trample Eric.

Arms stretched out at either side in order to make herself appear bigger, she called out to Prince Albert, "Whoa, boy! Stop!" She moved toward her horse's path, bringing Jojo with her.

As Taylor had hoped, Prince Albert broke down to a quick trot, though his nostrils still flared and his eyes were wide. As soon as he was close enough, she snatched his reins, yanking his head down to hers. "What's *wrong* with you?" she demanded, her voice filled with worry. She quickly untied the offending saddle, tossing it on the ground behind her.

Once she was sure Prince Albert had settled, Taylor hurried to Eric, one horse in each hand. Tears began to brim in her eyes as she almost tripped over herself, trying to reach him. Why wasn't he moving?

She knelt down next to him and tapped his shoulder. "Eric! Eric, wake up!" She had learned in health class to not shake the person if there was a suspected neck or back injury.

Eric lay on his side, his left shoulder twisted at a painful-looking angle. He had bloody scrapes down the side of his face where he had landed in the dirt. Letting go of the horses' reins, she knelt to hear if he was breathing.

Well, she thought he was . . . she wasn't absolutely sure. She put her hand on Eric's neck to find a pulse. She thought she felt movement against her palm.

Stay calm, Taylor commanded herself as she let go of Prince Albert's reins and reached into her front pocket to fish out her cell phone. *Call 911!*

Her finger was on the nine when Eric groaned and stirred. Eyelashes fluttering, he blinked a few times, trying to regain focus.

Taylor's trembling hands returned her phone to her pocket and clutched Prince Albert's reins, as well as Jojo's, once again. "Eric! Can you hear me? Are you all right?" she asked urgently, trying to steady her wavering voice. "You were passed out for almost a minute."

Eric moaned once more and seemed to be suddenly hit with a wave of pain. He sat up, a grimace on his face, and grabbed at his shoulder. Wincing, he looked at Taylor. "Is Prince Albert okay?" he asked, and coughed a few times, dirt falling off him.

Taylor bit back tears once again, touched that after being knocked unconscious his first worries were about her horse and not himself. "Yeah, he's fine," she squeaked, reaching out and brushing dirt off of his clothing. "But are you? You had a pretty bad fall."

"I think I'm okay. What happened?" he asked, rubbing his neck with the hand of his uninjured arm. "I was staying on fine until the saddle slipped, which spooked him, I guess. Did you remember to tighten the cinch when we got in the ring?"

"Yeah, of course I . . ." Her voice trailed off as a whole host of new emotions washed over her.

She *hadn't* tightened the cinch.

She had forgotten when she ran to get the helmets. "Oh, Eric, I'm so sorry!" she wailed, her face crumpling.

She leaned forward and wrapped her arms around him, burying her face into his dirty shirt. "I'm just so glad you're okay," she sobbed.

Eric flinched. "Watch the shoulder!" Then he softened. "It's okay. Mistakes happen. We're all fine."

Taylor nodded quietly and stood, holding her hand out to Eric to help him up. He grabbed it and hoisted himself up, wincing in pain. Taking hold of Jojo's reins, he began to hobble forward. Taylor stood for a moment, trying to regain her composure, while Eric headed back to the barn.

Just then, Beverly Mason sped up the drive at an alarming speed. *Great. What timing.* Taylor scowled to herself as the black SUV came to a skidding stop in front of the barn. A plume of dust washed over the limping Eric and Jojo.

Taylor watched as Plum stepped out of the car, velvet hunt cap under one arm, riding crop in the other. Her polished black tall boots contrasted starkly with Eric's dirtied appearance. "What happened to *you*?" Plum asked her cousin, blonde eyebrows raised in surprise.

Eric stopped and looked at her for a moment, seeming to consider his answer. He glanced back at Taylor, who still stood in the ring. He turned back to Plum. "Uh . . . I fell off of Jojo. He spooked at something, and I guess I just wasn't sitting right." He walked into the barn without any further explanation.

Plum laughed and followed after him, poking him in the back with her riding crop. "You *would* fall off. You're such a klutz sometimes." Their voices faded into the barn as Taylor began to trudge toward them, wiping the tears from her eyes. She looked back at Prince Albert sadly. She was beginning to think this would never work.

Prince Albert might always be a one-girl horse, and that would never do. But even if she had to give him up, where would he go? If no one else could ride him, no one else would want him. And Eric certainly wouldn't want to try again, what with her forgetting to tighten the cinch added to the fact that Prince Albert now seemed to think he was a bronco.

What was she going to do?

Mrs. LeFleur came hurrying out of the main building wearing an alarmed expression. "I just saw Eric pass by and he looks terrible. Did he fall from —"

She stopped short and took in Taylor's disheveled appearance. "You don't look so good, either," Mrs. LeFleur noted fretfully. "And . . . have you been crying? What happened out here?"

Taylor couldn't think fast enough to come up with something, and besides, she didn't like the idea of lying to Mrs. LeFleur. The entire story came spilling from her lips as she watched Mrs. LeFleur's anxious expression become increasingly alarmed. "How long was he completely unconscious?"

Closing her eyes, Taylor tried to calculate the time. She'd had to get hold of Prince Albert and settle him down, and then she'd crossed the ring and gotten her phone out. "A minute," she estimated uncertainly.

"Oh, dear," Mrs. LeFleur said with a gasp. "We have to get him to a doctor, make sure he's all right." Mrs. LeFleur hurried to Beverly Mason's SUV and rapped on the driver's side window.

The tinted glass window slid down, and Plum's mother gazed coolly at Mrs. LeFleur. "You have to get your nephew to a doctor," Mrs. LeFleur urged. "He's had a fall and been knocked unconscious. We can't take any chances."

"Oh, he seems fine to me," Beverly Mason said.

"You must take him right now!" Mrs. LeFleur insisted.

"I don't think so," Beverly Mason disagreed in a level, disdainful tone.

Taylor didn't know which of them was right. Eric did seem okay, yet she'd be inclined to trust Mrs. LeFleur's judgment over that of Plum's mother any day of the week. Mrs. LeFleur's panic seemed out of character, though.

"I insist he be taken to a doctor or to the emergency room," Mrs. LeFleur shouted. Taylor thought Mrs. LeFleur might even burst into tears. "If I have to, I will take him myself."

"Oh, fine, if you must," Mrs. Mason relented angrily. "Take him! Take him! This is ridiculous."

Mrs. LeFleur put her arm around Eric's shoulders and guided him toward her car. "I wonder if I should call an ambulance," she mused.

"No, please," Eric said. "I don't need an ambulance."

"Maybe not," Mrs. LeFleur allowed, "but I'm taking you to the hospital to be checked. Taylor, can you watch things until I return?"

"I'm coming," Taylor insisted, hurrying to Mrs. LeFleur's car.

Mrs. LeFleur looked at the horses in the corral. "All

right," she said to Taylor. "The horses will be all right until we come back. Let's go."

Even though she thought Mrs. LeFleur was over-reacting, Taylor trusted the woman completely and would never doubt her judgment.

Still . . . there was something odd about the way Mrs. LeFleur was acting.

Chapter 9

An hour later, Taylor sat beside Mrs. LeFleur on the orange plastic chairs in the waiting room attached to the emergency room of the Pheasant Valley Hospital.

"Good thing Eric's father was home," she commented to Mrs. LeFleur. Mr. Mason had rushed to the hospital when Mrs. LeFleur called him and was now inside with his son while a doctor checked Eric over.

The sound of Taylor's voice made Mrs. LeFleur startle, as though her thoughts had taken her someplace very far away and she had been abruptly called back.

"What? Oh . . . yes . . . it was. I think a parent or relative has to check a minor into a hospital if prior permission hasn't been given. So we couldn't have done it without him."

"Eric seemed all right, though."

Behind her thick glasses, Mrs. LeFleur's eyes closed, and she sighed deeply. "You can never be too careful."

Even though Eric's dad told Mrs. LeFleur and Taylor that they didn't have to wait, Mrs. LeFleur had insisted that she wouldn't leave until she heard about Eric's condition.

Taylor wondered why Mrs. LeFleur was so upset. Even Eric said he felt fine. Taylor felt so confident that he wasn't seriously injured — especially after Mr. Mason told them the doctor was almost positive Eric was okay — that she'd called her father to come pick her up to take her home. Taylor didn't quite understand why Mrs. LeFleur was insisting on staying.

"How are things going these days . . . for Wildwood, I mean?" Taylor asked after a few more minutes of silent waiting. She was searching for some conversational subject to pass the time, and the ranch's finances were a natural topic. They'd been tight from the start because the costs of refurbishing the long-abandoned ranch had been high. Mrs. LeFleur constantly worried about money, but Taylor hadn't heard her mention anything about it for a couple of weeks.

Taylor was hoping things were better now that they had the County HORSE contract. It also seemed like a good time to remind Mrs. LeFleur that they had the contract due to Prince Albert's excellent performance at the Rotary Show.

"We need more business," Mrs. LeFleur replied absently. She turned toward Taylor. "Do you think I'm overreacting to this?"

Taylor suddenly felt put on the spot. "Maybe a little . . . I don't know."

Just then a tall man with dark blond hair came through the automatic glass doors. He had obviously come straight from work since he still wore the coveralls of an auto mechanic. "Mrs. LeFleur!" Steve Henry cried fondly when he spotted her. "Good to see you!"

Mrs. LeFleur rose to give him a hug. "Little Stevie Henry!"

Taylor had heard Mrs. LeFleur call her father that before, and she always thought it was funny, especially since her father was well over six feet tall. Although Mrs. LeFleur remembered Taylor's father, this was the first time they were actually seeing each other in many years.

"It's been so long, but you look the same," Mrs. LeFleur said.

"So do you," Steve Henry replied.

"Nice of you to say so, even if it is a complete lie," Mrs. LeFleur said with a smile.

Taylor's father used to ride at Wildwood Stables back when Mrs. LeFleur's uncle ran the place. Her uncle was Devon Ross's father, and the two cousins had been brought up almost as sisters, since Mrs. LeFleur's parents had died when Mrs. LeFleur was a child. Her father had told Taylor that Mrs. LeFleur had been a champion rider back then, winning all sorts of awards, especially as a jumper.

"How's Jimmy?" Taylor's father asked. Jimmy, Taylor knew, was Mrs. LeFleur's son.

Mrs. LeFleur looked away as though the subject was painful. "You know he never walked again after the accident," she said stiffly.

"Yes, I knew he was in a wheelchair, but how is he?" Steve Henry said.

"We had a falling-out some years ago, and we haven't spoken since," Mrs. LeFleur divulged.

"A falling-out?" Taylor asked. She had never heard that expression before.

"A fight," Mrs. LeFleur explained. "Quite a bad fight."

The obvious question sprang to Taylor's lips. *What did you fight about?* But she didn't give voice to it. It seemed rude to ask.

"Ah, gee, I'm sorry to hear that," Steve said. "Maybe the two of you should get back in touch. I always liked Jimmy."

"Yes, well . . . It's very nice to see you again. I met your wife not long ago. She seemed lovely."

"She is. But actually she's my *ex*-wife," Steve said awkwardly.

Mrs. LeFleur looked to Taylor. "I'm sorry. I don't think Taylor ever told me her parents were divorced."

Taylor shrugged. "I guess it never came up." Taylor's parents had split up only six months earlier, and it wasn't something Taylor generally liked to talk about.

Steve seemed to really focus on his daughter for the first time. "You look a little roughed up, yourself. Did you fall, too?"

"No, but I was clinging on to a horse that bolted."

Steve scowled at her with a puzzled expression. "What crazy kind of riding were you two lunatics doing?"

"I'll tell you in the car."

"Sure you don't want a lift home, Mrs. LeFleur?" Steve offered.

"No, I have my car, thank you."

Taylor said good night and left with her father. "That must have brought back some bad memories for her," Steve commented as they headed out to the parking lot.

"Why?" Taylor asked.

"Jimmy LeFleur took a bad fall from his horse and —"

"Landed in a wheelchair for the rest of his life," Taylor filled in the rest. "I know. You told me."

Steve opened the car door for her and then went around to the driver's side and turned on the engine. "Yeah, but he seemed to be okay at first. I mean, he was unconscious for just a little while. But that night he went into a coma and didn't come out for a few days. When he did come out of it, there was damage to his spinal cord, and he never walked again. And I guess he never rode a horse again, either."

An image flashed into Taylor's head. It was of

the boy in the wheelchair from the County program. "Not necessarily," she disagreed. "People in wheelchairs can ride."

"That's true. I wonder if Jimmy ever did get back on a horse," Steve said.

"It's Mrs. LeFleur who never rode again," Taylor said.

That night Taylor lay on her bed wondering what Mrs. LeFleur had fought with her son about. How terrible it must be for Mrs. LeFleur to have a son she didn't see or even talk to. Wildwood's owner seemed so warm and kind; it was hard to believe she could hang on to a grudge against her own child. And, for that matter, her cousin. It seemed that Devon Ross was trying to make up with Mrs. LeFleur for some reason — she'd even donated Shafir to Wildwood Stables — but Mrs. LeFleur refused to have anything to do with her. Taylor found it very puzzling.

She was about to switch off the lamp on her night-stand when her cell phone buzzed. The name ERIC MASON came up, and Taylor's heart raced.

"Hi, Eric, how are you feeling?"

"I'm a little sore, that's all. I don't know why Mrs. LeFleur made such a big deal."

"I think I found out why," Taylor told him. "Your accident must have reminded Mrs. LeFleur of what happened to her son, Jimmy. He took a bad fall and never walked again."

There was silence on Eric's end of the phone. "Wow," he said seriously after a moment. "That's bad."

"I know," Taylor agreed somberly.

"I guess I'm lucky."

"Or Jimmy was unlucky. Everyone falls eventually," Taylor said.

"Yeah," Eric agreed. "That's true." There was more silence. "Well, listen, I have some good news," Eric said brightly, changing the mood of their conversation. "My friend called and said he could get us a whole bunch of horse shampoos and horse treats. He's even got some combs and brushes so you can replace some of the worn ones in your grooming kit."

"That's awesome," Taylor said, smiling. "And it's really free?"

"Not exactly, but I only had to give him twenty bucks for all of it."

"Then I'll pay you ten. We'll split it," Taylor offered.

"You don't have to."

Taylor was touched that he was willing to share with her, asking nothing in return. "No, I'll give you the ten. It's only fair to split the cost," she insisted.

"Sure, okay," he gave in. "But I have even better news. My friend has a pony blanket, and he thinks that the store will be getting rid of the inventory of old, unsold horse blankets next week."

A smile spread across Taylor's face. "Are you kidding?"

"No. That's what he told me."

Prince Albert wouldn't be shivering through the winter, after all!

"That's great. Thanks, Eric. Thanks so much!"

"No problem. Now, if we can only get our horses to behave, all our problems will be solved."

Chapter 10

On Friday, Taylor sat on the split-rail fence of the corral nearest the main building and watched Dana ride Prince Albert at a walk around the ring. Lois, her instructor, stayed at her side.

Dana put down the reins and spread her arms out at either side while Prince Albert kept walking.

"Wow," Taylor breathed, impressed. Beginners typically learned this move, that was true, yet it was an impressive accomplishment for Dana. The girl had autism and was often distracted. Spreading her arms wide while riding took concentration, confidence, and balance.

On solid ground, Dana was often unfocused, nervous, and uncoordinated — but not when she rode. Sitting atop

Prince Albert, Dana was always the picture of calm composure, and never more so than at that moment. Pride beamed from Dana's face, but she kept her chin up and her eyes straight ahead, gazing through Prince Albert's ears as Lois had instructed her.

"Good boy, Prince Albert," Taylor whispered as her horse, Dana, and Lois walked past. Hearing her voice, the quarter horse sputtered softly.

Taylor clapped her hand over her mouth. Maybe she shouldn't have spoken. It might not be wise to remind Prince Albert that he was carrying a rider other than Taylor. But the black horse clipclopped steadily on.

Daphne came and stood beside Taylor at the outside of the fence. Behind her, Pixie was saddled. The cream Shetland kept her eyes fixed on Prince Albert. She shifted uneasily from side to side. "Steady, there," Daphne cautioned the pony. "I know you're dying to follow your pal, but we have pony rides to give in fifteen minutes."

"Really?" Taylor asked.

"A whole birthday party of little kids will be arriving," Daphne confirmed. "I'm going to take them to the upper pasture so they don't bother Dana."

"Cool," Taylor said, knowing that any new business was good for Wildwood.

They watched together in silence for another minute as Prince Albert carried Dana along steadily. "He does well with Dana, doesn't he," Daphne remarked, her eyes following Prince Albert in the corral.

Nodding, Taylor turned toward her. "Why won't he do that with other riders?"

Daphne shook her head. "I don't know."

"It's as though he knows how much Dana loves and needs him," Taylor suggested. "She fell in love with Prince Albert the moment she saw him."

"I remember her first day here," Daphne recalled. "She wouldn't ride any other horse."

"I know."

The sound of hoofbeats coming from the stable made Daphne and Taylor turn. Looking elegant in her English riding gear, Plum rode Shafir out the front door. "Shafir's training is coming along well," Daphne noted. "She's such a good horse now. Remember what a wild filly she was when Mrs. Ross first sent her over to us?"

"I do remember," Taylor agreed. "You and Mercedes have done a great job training her."

"Thanks. The hardest part has been keeping Plum from ruining her."

"I hid her shank chain in some hay," Taylor said with a mischievous smile.

Daphne grinned. "Oh, good for you! I can just picture her looking everywhere for it. You're hilarious."

"I hate that thing," Taylor added seriously. The shank chain was a chain added to the mouthpiece of a halter used to yank a horse's head down if the animal won't behave. Taylor supposed it might have its place in the training of a difficult horse, but Plum used it to excess, and she pulled hard and abruptly. Whenever she pulled the chain on lovely, high-spirited Shafir, Taylor could barely control her anger.

Two minivans pulled in and both were filled with four- and five-year-old boys and girls. "I could use some help with these guys. Are you doing anything?" Daphne asked.

"No. I'll go get a helmet and meet you up in the pasture. I hope Plum isn't riding up there."

"Speaking of Plum, I wonder if she said something to upset Mercedes," Daphne mentioned.

"Why do you say that?"

"I just left Mercedes in the stable watering the horses, and she looks all bummed. When I asked what was wrong, she just told me it was nothing."

"Typical Mercedes." The girl had always been pretty secretive.

"I know," Daphne agreed.

Taylor leaped lightly down from the fence. "I'll see what I can find out," she said, heading toward the main building that housed the stable.

As Taylor entered the shady coolness of the stable's central aisle, she breathed in the musky smell of horse sweat and droppings mingled with the scent of hay. It was an odor she adored because it meant she was at Wildwood Stables, her favorite place on earth.

Glancing to her left, Taylor saw Mrs. LeFleur in her office studying a large notebook of the ranch's accounts. She didn't look happy. Taylor wished things were easier for Mrs. LeFleur. Why couldn't she be wealthy like her cousin Devon Ross? It didn't seem fair.

A few paces farther down, she stuck her head into the tack room and grabbed a velvet riding helmet from a hook. She smiled at Spots. The tiny fawn slept contentedly, its spindly legs tucked underneath its belly.

Stepping out of the tack room once again, Taylor checked around for Mercedes but didn't see her anywhere.

Then she heard a sniffling sound coming from Prince Albert's stall.

Following it, she found Mercedes sitting on the stall floor with her head down. It took a moment for Taylor to realize that Mercedes was crying. Taylor knew Mercedes would be embarrassed to be discovered like this; she always put up such a tough exterior. Taylor intentionally kicked the side of the stable with her riding boot to give the girl warning that she was there.

"Who's there?" Mercedes asked in an unsteady voice.

It surprised Taylor that Mercedes wasn't even attempting to cover up the tears in her voice.

"It's just me. Are you okay?" she asked.

Mercedes didn't answer. Taylor heard another sniff as she went into Prince Albert's stall. She sat on the straw-covered floor beside Mercedes. "Did Plum do something?" she asked gently.

With her eyes fixed on the ground, Mercedes nodded. "Her mother is thinking of buying Monty for her."

"Where did you hear that?" Taylor asked.

"Mom got a call from Devon Ross last night. It seems Monty's registration papers have been lost, and she wanted to know if my mother has a copy of them."

"Does she?" Taylor asked.

Mercedes shook her head. "No. I took them."

"You have them?"

"Yeah. But Mom doesn't know. She's been looking everywhere."

"You're not going to tell her you have them?"

"If I don't tell her it will slow down the process of buying Monty."

"Can't she trace Monty's registration through the Fox Trotting Association?"

"Probably," Mercedes agreed. "But I'm going to do anything I can to delay this." Her face scrunched into an expression of deep unhappiness. "Oh, Taylor, I couldn't stand to see her on Monty. It's bad enough we have to watch her push Shafir and hit her and not groom her properly. Even if she treated Monty well, I couldn't bear to see her on him."

"Did Mrs. Ross tell your mom that she was definitely selling Monty to Plum's mother?" Taylor asked.

101

Mercedes looked up thoughtfully. "Not exactly, I guess, but she must be selling him. Why else would she need his papers?"

"Lots of reasons," Taylor said, brightening. "Why would you think it was Plum who wanted Monty?"

"Because she told me just now." Mercedes nodded sadly. "Plum said her mother was there the other day to look at Monty. Remember? We saw her. That's why they had you ride him."

"Well, I'm sure I didn't show him off too well," Taylor said, trying to be encouraging. "I'm such a beginner at English style. I could make even the best horse look bad."

"Thanks, but you did fine. And — no offense — but Monty could make even the worst rider look good. You know how great he is," Mercedes replied.

Taylor knew it was true. Monty was, by nature, a smart and responsive horse, and Mercedes had trained him beautifully. "If she buys Monty, Plum might board him here. That would be a good thing, wouldn't it?" Taylor offered as a possible consolation.

Mercedes stood, brushing straw from her jeans. "No, it wouldn't. I couldn't stand to see it."

"You could protect him from her, watch over him," Taylor insisted. She knew how Mercedes felt, though. When she'd thought Plum was going to buy Prince Albert she'd been almost sick with worry. "Shafir is doing all right even though she's leasing him," Taylor reminded Mercedes. "We're making sure Plum doesn't ride her too hard, and if she doesn't groom her properly we do it."

"Plum still mistreats Shafir," Mercedes grumbled. "Look, I know I said I'd work with you on your jumping, but I've got to get out of here. If I run into Plum again . . . it won't be good."

"What would you do?" Taylor asked nervously.

"I don't know. That's why I have to leave."

Chapter 11

Up you go," Taylor sang out as she swung a small boy with wild blond curly hair into Pixie's saddle. "Hold on to the saddle."

Daphne stood at Pixie's head holding the reins. "Ready?" she asked the boy.

"The pony looks like me," he noted happily. "We have the same hair."

"Yes, you do," Taylor agreed. She smiled and stroked Pixie's frizzy white-blonde mane. "Look at that."

"That's funny," Daphne said, yawning widely.

"Are you getting tired?" Taylor asked. This was the seventh of the eleven young party guests to take a walking tour of the pasture astride Pixie. "I could take him around while you stay with the kids."

"Honestly, I could use a break," Daphne admitted. "What are you doing with them while they wait?"

Taylor came forward and took the reins from Daphne. "I'm telling them facts about horses, but they're really little, so I'm also having them pretend to trot around and make clopping noises with their mouths and hands."

Daphne rolled her eyes as she smiled. "On second thought, I think it might be easier to take Pixie around the pasture."

"Too late," Taylor teased with a laugh. "I have the reins now."

"I'll remember that. You tricked me," Daphne said as she headed toward the rest of the party. An anxious-looking mother of the birthday girl nervously tried to keep all the guests together in a group.

"Okay, here we go," Taylor told the boy in the saddle. "We're taking a pony ride." She turned her attention to Pixie and clucked. "Walk on, girl."

The little Shetland moved forward obediently as Taylor led her in a wide oval path around the pasture. A breeze swept across the rough grass, causing a ripple. For a moment it reminded Taylor of the surface of nearby Mohegan Lake when a wind crossed it. The red and orange leaves on the trees in the woods beyond the pasture were also stirred by the chilly air current and made Taylor aware of the nip in the air.

This morning before she left the house, Taylor had tucked a yellow hand-knit scarf into the neckline of her jean jacket. Now she took a moment to pull it more tightly around her neck. The weather was changing fast. If it was this cool now, what would the night be like?

The stable wasn't heated. Of course the body heat from the other horses and the warmth from the hay would keep the cold off for a while. And the horses were sheltered from the wind.

Taylor knew that horses in the wild lived outside and endured long, cold winters in some places. But Pixie and Prince Albert weren't wild. And Pixie was an older pony. She didn't like to think of them shivering, uncovered in their stalls. If only she had a job that paid money — but then, when would she have the time to work at Wildwood Stables as partial payment for their board?

Smiling at the boy in the all-purpose saddle, Taylor checked that he was holding the front of it tightly and wasn't sliding. "Having fun?" she asked.

The boy's head bobbed up and down gleefully.

With a nod, Taylor glanced at Daphne and smiled at the line of galloping preschoolers that Daphne was leading. Leading Pixie was definitely the easier job.

Taylor had nearly completed her course when she saw Eric approaching the field on Jojo. They cantered up to the fence near Taylor. "I got some great horse stuff from my friend," he told Taylor excitedly. "When you're finished here, come down to the stable. I have a surprise for you."

"This is too awesome!" Taylor said as she ripped open the cellophane wrapper covering a blue-and-purple-plaid horse blanket. "Are you sure you only paid ten dollars for this?"

"Yep," Eric confirmed with a satisfied grin.

"Wow!" Taylor spread the horse sheet out across the door of Prince Albert's stall. "He'll be warm in this. Thanks so much for getting it. Can I pay you tomorrow? I have the money at home."

Next to Prince Albert's stall she'd spread out the smaller gray blanket Eric had brought for Pixie. He'd also bought horse shampoo, treats, vitamins, and a hoof cream. "I can't believe they were getting rid of all this," Taylor mused.

"My friend said they have to make way for new inventory, so they sell it to the employees cheap, and he sells it to me for the price he pays," Eric explained.

"It's lucky to have a friend like that," Taylor said as she screwed open a bottle of the shampoo and sniffed it. Liking the smell, she wondered if it would work well on her own hair. She'd heard some riders say that they used horse shampoo on themselves.

Eric reached into the large plastic bag he'd brought the new horse items in. "I know you're insisting on paying for your share of everything else," he said, "but not this." He pulled a large box from the bag. "This is from me to you."

A present? Eric had gotten her a gift?

Taylor fought against the color she felt rising in her cheeks. From the heat on her face, she suspected she was losing the battle.

Eric handed her the box. "It's no big deal," he said, not meeting her gaze.

"A new grooming kit," Taylor cried, examining the box. An expression of delight swept her face. "You knew I needed this."

"Yeah," Eric agreed.

"I should pay you for this," Taylor said, suddenly feeling awkward. He'd gotten her a gift, and it wasn't her birthday or anything.

"I said it was from me to you," Eric insisted, still not meeting her eyes. "Besides, I got it at a . . . you know . . . a discount."

"Still . . ." Taylor waited for him to look at her. "Thank you. Thanks a lot."

They looked at each other for another moment that felt much longer than it was. The corners of Eric's mouth turned up into a slight smile.

"Prince Albert is done with his lesson," Eric said at last, turning toward the open door at the front of the stable. "And Jojo is still saddled. Want to work with them some more?"

Taylor was happy to hear him speak as if nothing had happened. "Sure," she said, setting down the grooming kit. "But aren't you — aren't you nervous . . . after what happened last time and all?"

Eric grinned. "I don't mind falling. The only thing that has me nervous is Mrs. LeFleur making a big deal over it again."

That made Taylor smile. "She was just concerned."

"I know."

"Mercedes was going to work with me on my jumps this afternoon, but she had to go home," Taylor said.

"That's right. The event is this weekend, isn't it?" Eric recalled. "Do you feel ready for it?"

"Not exactly. But I've been practicing, and I haven't knocked down any of the rails all this week."

"Would you rather practice now?" Eric asked.

It occurred to Taylor that maybe she ought to be practicing, but she'd so much rather be doing something with Eric. "No. Let's work with Prince Albert and Jojo while we're both here," Taylor said, and they started walking toward the front. "We have to think of some way to get them to cooperate."

"But how?" Eric asked. "I went online to see if I could learn something about this problem, but I couldn't find anything."

"Daphne once showed me that if you breathe into

a horse's nostrils the horse gets to know you," Taylor suggested.

"All right," Eric said. "We can try that first. It might even settle Prince Albert down about not liking guys."

"I don't know," Taylor said doubtfully. "I'd hate for you to get hurt again."

"I won't," Eric said. "But I'm definitely wearing a helmet, just in case. You should, too."

"I always do," Taylor said honestly.

They went to the tack room to find helmets and then headed outside. Jojo, Prince Albert, and Pixie were all in the corral, still saddled and grazing on patches of higher grass that grew around the fence posts. Eric approached Prince Albert and glanced over at Taylor. "Do we just stand in front and breathe?" he checked.

"Yeah," Taylor confirmed as she walked around to face Jojo. "That's all that Daphne did. But maybe we should pet them a bit first."

Taylor swept her hand along Jojo's broad flank. "Hi, big fella," she crooned gently. "It's me, Taylor. You've seen me around. I want us to be friends. Do you think I could ride you today? Would that be all right? I'm Eric's friend, and he says it's all right with him."

Prince Albert's frenzied whinny drew Taylor's attention from Jojo. Her horse danced away from Eric's attempts to pet him. He stomped his front hoofs in an intimidating protest whenever Eric tried to approach him.

"Prince Albert! Stop!" Taylor scolded firmly. She turned to Eric. "This isn't going to work," she said. "He was all right with you as long as you didn't try to touch him."

Before Eric could reply, they were both distracted by the sound of an approaching car. It was actually two cars, one following behind the other, and she thought she recognized the second car.

It was Devon Ross's sporty BMW.

Chapter 12

Taylor glanced over to Eric and their eyes met, silently asking the same question. What was Devon Ross doing at Wildwood Stables?

The driver of the first car — a silver van — parked along the round corral but didn't get out.

Devon Ross pulled up to the main building and threw open the driver's side door. The tall, thin woman was elegantly dressed in a beige pantsuit with a brown suede jacket over her shoulders. Her dark hair was pulled back severely from her angular face and clasped at the nape of her neck. It was the only style Taylor had ever seen her wear. The owner of Ross River Ranch strode into the main building with confidence.

What was going on? Taylor burned to know.

Could she go into the office on some pretext to eaves-drop? Maybe she'd hear a snippet of conversation that would reveal what was happening.

Taylor peered through the lightly tinted glass of the parked van. A man's form was visible in the driver's seat, but she couldn't see him clearly. He was reaching into the backseat for something.

Eric was also trying to see into the vehicle's window. Turning back to Taylor, he shrugged. "Want to do the breathing thing now?" he asked, apparently having lost interest in the visitors.

With a nod of agreement, Taylor turned to face Jojo. After running her hand comfortingly down his muzzle and speaking to him soothingly, Taylor inhaled deeply. Jojo's nostrils flared slightly as Taylor blew softly into them. His ears perked forward with interest. "That's a good boy," Taylor praised him. "We can be friends."

Almost as if he'd overheard her, Prince Albert swung his head toward Taylor, pulling away from Eric again. Inwardly, Taylor cringed at the look of betrayal she thought she detected in her horse's soulful dark eyes. "A person can have more than one friend," she stated firmly, addressing what she was sure was his unspoken accusation.

"Not as far as he's concerned."

Taylor turned toward the voice that had spoken from just outside the corral.

Prince Albert sputtered unhappily, registering his unease in the presence of men, especially an unfamiliar one. "Easy, boy," Eric soothed him.

The man sat in a wheelchair, and Taylor realized he must be the driver of the van. She saw that crutches lay across the wheelchair's arms and was impressed that he'd obviously gotten himself out of the van and into his wheelchair without help. Taking in his dark blond hair and round face, Taylor felt positive that he had to be Jimmy LeFleur.

"Lend him your scarf," the man suggested.

Taylor fingered the yellow scarf at her throat. "This?"

"Yeah," the man confirmed. "Let your friend wear it. Let that other horse graze awhile. And you come stand here by the black horse."

Eric turned toward the man. "We're trying to get him to accept me as a rider when the only one he wants to ride him is —"

"Yeah, yeah," the man said quickly, cutting Eric off with a touch of impatience. "I figured that out."

Taylor wrapped her scarf around Eric's neck.

"Good," the man prompted. "That scarf has your scent on it. What's the horse's name?"

"Prince Albert," Taylor told him. "And I'm Taylor and he's Eric."

"Hi. I'm Jim."

I knew it! Taylor thought triumphantly. It *was* Mrs. LeFleur's son!

"Okay," Jim went on. "Now stand beside Eric while he does the breathing thing. That's what you guys were about to do, wasn't it?"

"Yeah," Eric confirmed. He and Taylor faced Prince Albert. When Eric stroked his forelock, Prince Albert whinnied and shifted uneasily. "It's okay, boy," Taylor said gently.

"Keep talking, and you pet him, too," Jim coached.

Taylor soothed Prince Albert with soft words of encouragement while she and Eric touched his sides and muzzle. "Okay, Eric, while Taylor keeps talking, you breathe into the big guy's nostrils," Jim instructed.

They stayed that way with Taylor crooning to her horse and Eric breathing for almost ten more minutes. Prince Albert sputtered into Eric's face, causing the boy to screw up his features as he wiped off the spray. "Don't stop breathing," Jim called.

After another few minutes, Jim told Eric to climb onto Prince Albert's back. "You stay right in front of him, Taylor," Jim added.

Eric stuck his foot in the stirrups and swung up into the saddle.

Prince Albert nickered uneasily.

Taylor's eyes darted nervously to Jim. What should they do? Would Prince Albert throw Eric again?

"Take the reins and walk him, Taylor. Be very firm with him," Jim advised.

With a nod to Jim, Taylor clicked for Prince Albert to walk. Prince Albert neighed and pulled back. "Walk on, boy. Right now. Walk on," Taylor commanded.

Prince Albert stepped forward, and soon Taylor was walking him around the corral with Eric on his back. When she was about to pass Jim, Taylor looked to him for more instruction.

"Keep going," he said. "You're doing great. Just keep going around and around."

"Can we stop now?" Taylor asked after she'd been walking for another ten minutes.

Jim shook his head. "Keep going."

As Taylor walked she noticed Mrs. LeFleur and Devon Ross coming out of the main building. They weren't arguing, but both women scowled and spoke to each other seriously. Again, Taylor longed to know what they were saying.

"Now pass Eric the reins and slowly back away," Jim told Taylor when she passed him again.

Prince Albert whinnied anxiously when Taylor stepped back four paces. She glanced to Jim for advice. "Keep going, but slow," he said.

Prince Albert kept an eye on Taylor as she made her way painstakingly to the fence. Jojo picked up his head and neighed.

Taylor could barely breathe as she leaned into the fence and watched Eric ride Prince Albert at a steady walk. They made it around the ring once . . . twice. . . .

"Now take him to a trot," Jim called.

Taylor swung her head around to look at him questioningly. Was it too soon for this?

Jim's reply was to jut his chin toward the ring. Taylor turned to see Eric riding Prince Albert at a smooth trot. She smiled with relief. It really seemed to be working.

Not only was Prince Albert accepting a new rider — but he was allowing a male to ride him!

Impossible!

Amazing!

Taylor turned toward Jim LeFleur. "He usually hates men," she informed him.

"It's okay. He'll get over that as long as he smells your scent. It's like you've given your approval. The new rider has been marked as part of your herd."

Taylor looked at Jim LeFleur with admiration. "Are you a horse whisperer?" she asked. She had read about people who related to horses astoundingly well based on their deep understanding of how horses thought and felt.

Jim LeFleur smiled. "I'm flattered you think so. No, I've just been around horses all my life, and I know them. Maybe that does make me a horse whisperer of sorts. That horse doesn't hate men, he's just afraid of them. If you tell him this guy is okay, your horse will believe you. It's clear he's devoted to you."

Taylor watched Eric ride for a few minutes before turning back to Jim. She was about to once more say how amazed and thrilled and grateful she was, but she snapped her mouth shut when Mrs. LeFleur appeared beside Jim, staring at him angrily.

Taylor stayed quiet so she wouldn't miss a word.

"So, I hear you're working for Aunt Devon now," Mrs. LeFleur said with a note of accusation in her tone.

"Yes, I am, Mom. Do you have a problem with that?" Jim asked.

"I might," Mrs. LeFleur said coldly. "But I suspect you already knew that."

"Aunt Devon offered me a job. I needed one. I just wasn't ready to move to Kentucky."

"There are a lot of other people you could have gone to work for," Mrs. LeFleur said, her voice rising with anger.

"I couldn't find any jobs that were available," Jim replied. "Were you and Aunt Devon able to come to an agreement?"

Mrs. LeFleur folded her arms and turned away. "I'm still thinking about it."

Jim nodded. "Well, don't take too long. There are other people we can go to, you know."

Mrs. LeFleur looked at him once more. "Good to see you, Jim. You're looking well," she said stiffly before heading back toward the main building.

"Same to you, Mother," Jim mumbled even though Mrs. LeFleur had gone out of hearing distance.

Taylor took a moment to absorb what she'd heard. So Jim hadn't stopped being involved with horses, not even after his fall. He obviously knew what he was talking about, too.

He sat there lost in his own thoughts until Taylor coughed to get his attention. "Should we do the same thing with Jojo?" she asked him.

He looked at her as though he didn't understand.

"The other horse," Taylor explained. "He'll only let Eric ride him."

"Oh, yeah. Sure. You wear something Eric has worn, and you guys try the same approach I showed you." Turning his wheelchair toward his van, he reached into his pocket and tossed Taylor a horse treat. "Be sure to reward Prince Albert."

"Thanks! Thanks so much for your help," Taylor said.

Jim waved as he continued toward his van. "Good luck!"

Eric came to a halt alongside her. Taylor nuzzled Prince Albert, stroking his mane. "What a good, good boy you are." She held the treat to his lips, and he eagerly lapped it up.

"Success," Eric cried as he dismounted. "What a smart guy!"

"He's Mrs. LeFleur's son," she told Eric.

"No way! Really? Yeah, the guy in the wheelchair! I remember now."

"He's working at Ross River," Taylor added.

"I wonder how Mrs. LeFleur feels about that."

"Not great," Taylor said. "I heard them talking."

"Hey, listen, I feel bad that you're not getting to practice."

"But we need to work with Jojo," Taylor reminded Eric.

"It can wait for another day. Why don't I set up

some rails? I know some about jumping. I could work with you."

"That would be awesome! I have to get some practice time in. The Gypsy Trails event is this Saturday, and I am nowhere near ready!"

Chapter 13

On Saturday Taylor was at Wildwood by six a.m. getting the horses ready and doing barn chores before the big show at Gypsy Trails. Show days always started before the sun came up and ended well after it set.

She, Eric, Mercedes, Daphne, Mrs. LeFleur, and even Plum all pitched in to get as many barn chores done as possible before leaving. Then they loaded the horses up, gathered their gear, and hit the road.

Daphne, Eric, and Mercedes went with Mr. Chang in his car. Taylor was dying to squeeze in with them but took pity on Mrs. LeFleur, who would be driving the horse trailer alone with Plum. She glumly headed toward the front of the horse trailer and climbed into the front seat, followed shortly by her competition.

They drove in silence through the sleepy streets of Pheasant Valley until they were just out of town and about to turn on the highway. "I have to get my half-skim, half-soy, venti mocha latte, or else I just can't compete today," Plum insisted as they were about to pass a fancy coffee shop.

"Are you kidding me, Plum?" Taylor griped. "We don't want to stop now."

"I have to have it," Plum said. "Mrs. LeFleur, please pull in."

"Plum, I can't park this trailer in that crowded parking lot, and we really don't have time," Mrs. LeFleur told her. "How about the drive-through just ahead?"

Plum sighed. "They don't have exactly what I want, but I suppose so." As they pulled in, Taylor giggled at the absurdity of a horse trailer in the drive-through lane, the people inside staring wide-eyed and confused.

When they finally arrived at the Gypsy Trails barn, the sun was creeping into the sky, spilling a soft purple light on the show grounds as the trailer rumbled to a stop amid a cloud of dust.

Plum was the first to pop out of the truck, sipping her iced coffee with a look of disdain. "Ugh. I think I'm allergic to the cheap stuff. I can feel myself breaking out in hives." She opened her cup and spilled its melted contents on the ground.

Taylor came out of the truck, scowled at Plum, but decided to ignore her. Eric, Mercedes, and Daphne were already there. Taylor joined them as they went around back to unload the horses from the trailer.

Mrs. LeFleur and Plum came around to join them. "I'm going to go check you all in for your respective classes and get your numbers," Mrs. LeFleur told the group. "After you unload the horses, give them some water, and let them stretch their legs for a bit, okay?"

Plum was busy shining her tall boots and barely seemed to hear Mrs. LeFleur.

"Let's see, Daphne and Mercedes, you're both in the advanced over fences group, and Plum and Taylor, you're in the beginner-novice over fences, correct?" Mrs. LeFleur asked, checking her registration form. The girls all nodded, and Mrs. LeFleur made some scratch marks, erasing something from the registration forms.

"Plum, why are you in the beginner group again?

You've competed at much higher levels." Mrs. LeFleur squinted at the form, making sure she had written the correct information.

"Shafir could use the practice. Lower levels are great for her to warm up to the show season with, after all," Plum said smugly, cocking her head at Taylor.

Taylor turned and stared at Eric, as if to say *Do you see this? Do you?!* Eric just shook his head as he stuffed some hay into the feeder for Jojo. Mrs. LeFleur shrugged and walked off toward the registration booth.

Mercedes and Daphne were grooming the horses on the other side of the trailer, getting them show ready, and Taylor joined them. It had taken hours this morning to braid and pull all of the horses' manes into neat little clusters in an even row. It had paid off, though — all the horses looked elegant and clean. Daphne called out to Plum as she picked up Mandy's leg. "Aren't you going to groom Shafir?" she asked, bending over the horse's large hooves.

Plum just shrugged. "I'll get to it. I groomed her just before we left," she said, picking at a cuticle.

"Well, just so you know, it's good practice to groom before and after. Grooming helps you give the horse a once-over and check for any cuts or swelling," Daphne said as she picked out a small piece of rock from Mandy's hoof. "And you want to remove anything that gets lodged in their feet during the trip."

Plum shrugged again and began to walk away. "Yeah, that's true. I'm going to go see if the breakfast vendor is open yet."

Mercedes looked up from braiding Mandy's tail as Plum walked away. "You're going to need to get back here and groom soon anyway," she shouted pointedly to Plum.

Without turning, Plum continued on toward the vendor's cart. Taylor couldn't tell if Plum was too far away to hear Mercedes or was simply acting as if she hadn't.

Mercedes gritted her teeth and mumbled something under her breath.

"I know," Taylor agreed, shaking her head ruefully. "Whatever you just said, the same goes for me."

About an hour went by as they continued to ready the horses. "I have to go," Daphne said, checking the time on her cell phone. "I'm a judge in this first event."

"I want to see the little kids, too," Taylor said, hitching Prince Albert to a rail. "They're so cute."

Mercedes and Taylor followed Daphne down to the ring to watch the mini stirrup class get led around by older riders. "This is more of a cuteness competition," Mercedes remarked as though she disapproved.

Taylor didn't care. She loved watching the little girls in their tiny hunt vests and their hair in braids and bows. They made Taylor say "awww" with each lap. Their ponies trotted around the ring, the person leading each girl barely at a jog herself.

"How can Daphne ever judge these guys?" Taylor wondered aloud.

Daphne awarded the first place ribbon to a girl with big blue eyes and pink bows in her and her pony's hair.

"Well, that was difficult," Daphne joked when the last ribbon had been given out and the little girls had left. "Now I'm free until my event."

The three girls went back up the hill to where the trailer and the horses were. Taylor walked around to the far side of the truck, planning on changing into her show clothing. It was almost time for Plum and her to start warming up, since their division was starting soon. Although she had no idea where Plum was, she didn't want to be late.

Two men in jeans and T-shirts approached her. One of the men stuffed a notepad into his back pocket and said something to the other man, who nodded in agreement and looked over at Mrs. LeFleur's trailer.

Reporters, maybe?

Taylor brightened at the idea. If she won, she would probably be in the newspaper! She smoothed back her hair and smiled brightly as the men came closer.

"Hi!" she said, flashing her best smile.

"Hello, I'm Inspector McCarey and this is Inspector Carter." He lifted his badge and identification card to her.

Taylor's brows shot up in surprise. Cops?

"We're here looking into a lead we've received as to the whereabouts of some stolen horse goods. Have you seen or heard of any recent suspicious activity lately, in regards to blankets, grooming materials, or anything of the sort?"

"Um . . . no, I don't think so," Taylor said uncertainly. Stolen horse goods? Why were they asking her?

Inspector McCarey looked toward the trailer where Prince Albert was munching peacefully on some grass. "You wouldn't mind if we had a look around, would you?" he asked, eyes fixed on where Prince Albert was standing.

"Uh . . . yeah, sure, go ahead, I guess." Taylor said, shrugging in response. She hadn't done anything wrong, so she didn't see the harm in letting the officers look around. "What exactly are you looking for?"

"About ten Kensington turnout sheets, a few Collegiate English saddles, some Oster grooming items, and some other stuff that was stolen from PetWorld." The officer paused and strode over toward Prince Albert. Taylor shot up from where she was resting against the truck and hurried after him, not sure what his sudden interest in her horse might be.

"In fact, sheets that looked a lot like this one," he said, reaching out and fingering the blanket Prince Albert was wearing. The gelding lifted his head and looked at the new person, nostrils flaring and taking in the unfamiliar scent.

Taylor hurried over next to them. She didn't want Prince Albert freaking out on the detective. "You'd better not touch him," she warned. "He doesn't like men."

Inspector McCarey gazed at her quizzically but backed away from Prince Albert. "As I was saying, where did you get this horse sheet or blanket or whatever you call it?"

"A lot of people here have turnout sheets like this," Taylor pointed out. "I mean, it's a horse show."

"Looks pretty new. No stains or anything yet," the detective remarked, glancing over Prince Albert's body. "When did you get it?"

"A few days ago . . ." Taylor said, trailing off at the end as she realized how suspicious this was all making her sound.

"May I ask from where?" Inspector Carter pressed, taking out the notepad and pencil.

"U-u-um," Taylor stammered. If his friend was the one who had stolen all of the blankets and tack, Eric could be in big trouble. And so could she! "Um," Taylor murmured once more. What should she say?

"I'm sorry, I couldn't hear you," Inspector Carter said, leaning in toward Taylor. Taylor's eyes cut from Prince Albert's blanket to the officers and back again.

"Um, yeah, some guy came around our barn selling stuff out of his trunk. He was selling it really cheap, and I didn't have a lot of money, so I didn't ask where he got it from," Taylor said, feeling the blood drain from her face as she lied to the officers.

Inspector McCarey raised his eyebrows. "And did you get a good look at this man?" he asked.

"No," Taylor said slowly. "He was . . . uh . . . taller than me and had . . . brown hair."

The officer shot Taylor an incredulous look, pen paused and hovering over his notepad. "Taller than *you* and had brown hair. That all?"

Taylor nodded vigorously, lips pursed together. The officer stared at her, clearly suspecting that she was being intentionally vague.

"Are you sure?" he asked slowly.

Taylor nodded quickly again.

"Right. Well" — Inspector McCarey and Inspector Carter looked dubiously at each other — "would you mind if we exchanged information? You know, just in case you would like to let us know anything."

"Sure, yeah, that's fine," Taylor squeaked. With a trembling hand, Taylor wrote out her name, address, and phone number for the police officer.

"Thank you for your help," Inspector Carter said. "I'm *sure* we'll be in touch."

Taylor gulped and stared as the two men departed, walking back down the hill. He was *sure*? What did that mean? She was hoping it was just a turn of phrase, but couldn't be certain.

Glancing down at her watch, Taylor jumped. It was almost time for her division! Quickly, she finished grooming Albert and threw his tack on with lightning speed. She grabbed Albert's reins and jogged down the hill toward the show ring, panting as she reached the group of people watching an equitation class.

Looking around to see where the rest of her group was, Taylor spotted only Plum, who was sitting under a tree, polishing her tall boots again. Shafir grazed next to her, fully tacked, reins dragging on the ground. Taylor huffed over to the duo, clutching at a stitch in her side.

"Shouldn't you pick up Shafir's reins?" Taylor said, massaging the stitch of pain that had come into her side from running. "You don't want her stepping into them; that could be really dangerous."

Plum shrugged, ignoring Taylor, looking far more interested in getting the perfect shine on her boots. "She'll be fine," Plum said, holding the boots at arm's length to better view her work.

Not wanting an argument, Taylor reached down and tossed the reins over Shafir's neck, glowering at Plum.

"C'mon, we're next," Taylor said. "And what bridle is this?" She knew she'd never seen Shafir's gleaming new bridle at the stable. "Is it new?"

"Yeah, Eric got it for me from one of his friends. Trying a new bit, too. Maybe it'll make this brat listen better." Plum said, standing and thumping Shafir on the neck.

Taylor wondered about Eric's friend and all of these new items springing up. Was it coincidence, or were all of these new things really stolen goods?

Chapter 14

Static rumbled from the loudspeaker, making Prince Albert and Shafir lift their heads high into the air, alert to any coming noise. "Class 12B, beginner-novice over fences, equitation class can mount up," a man's voice boomed.

"That's us," Taylor said, taking a deep breath. She turned and began to walk toward the gate. A wave of stress swept over her when she realized she would be in the show pen within five minutes. As she hurried toward the in gate, Prince Albert trotting along next to her, a voice to her right made her jump.

"Good luck, Taylor," said Keith Hobbes, who was standing next to Mrs. LeFleur and Plum's mother, leaning on the white fence that lined the show ring.

Beverly Mason nodded primly toward Taylor, not saying a word. Taylor smiled with tight politeness in reply, taking a deep breath.

Keith scanned Prince Albert's face and frowned. "You're really going to need luck if you go into the show ring like that," Keith stated, reaching forward and tucking Prince Albert's noseband in and tightening it. Then he reached over and buckled the horse's throatlatch.

Taylor's face burned with embarrassment as she realized that she had completely forgotten to do anything else besides actually putting the bridle on. Keith looked at the saddle. "And are your stirrups even? Looks like you're going to be riding a bit cockeyed there."

Taylor turned around and looked at her stirrups. One was on the smallest hole, while the other was about halfway down. "Oh, yeah, I should fix that," Taylor said absently, reaching forward and adjusting her stirrups.

How embarrassing! She couldn't believe she'd been so thoughtless. Those police officers had really shaken her concentration.

Keith put a hand on her shoulder and leaned down to look at her. "Are you sure you're ready to do this?" he asked kindly.

"Of course I am!" Taylor almost shouted. "Today has just been . . . weird. I'll be fine, thank you."

Keith pursed his lips together, seeming to assess Taylor with his gaze. He nodded and stood up. "Well, go get 'em. Remember, stay relaxed, keep your shoulders back, chin up, heels down, but most importantly" — he paused for dramatic effect and grinned as he added — "have fun with it."

His encouraging words and good spirits made Taylor smile. She was already feeling a little less nervous and a bit more confident. "Thank you," she said sincerely, "I will."

"Now entering the ring, rider number 582. On deck is rider number 194," the voice behind the speakers boomed forth.

Taylor looked over to the gate where Plum, number 194, was mounting Shafir. Grabbing hold of the reins, she yanked Shafir's head down. The Arabian tossed her head in the air and backpedaled, trying to move away from Plum's harsh handling.

Taylor winced and turned away to watch the other rider finish. She wanted to concentrate on the course, but her mind wandered back to her experience with the police. Would she have to give Prince Albert's blanket back if it turned out that it was one of the stolen ones? If so, how would she afford a new one? Would she get into trouble? Would the police think she had anything to do with the theft?

Taylor couldn't believe Eric would have anything to do with buying stolen goods. How well did she really know him, though? Was it possible?

"Now entering the ring is rider number 194, on deck is number 845," the announcer called out as the rider who had just competed exited the ring, petting her horse on the neck as she left. Taylor looked toward his voice booming from the public address speaker. Plum was number 194 and Taylor was 845. They were up next.

Plum straightened up and kicked Shafir into a trot to enter the ring for her courtesy circle. As soon as it was over, she kicked Shafir up into a canter, heading toward the first jump.

Shafir pranced, head held high, eyes wide. The lovely young mare was ready to jump. In fact, Shafir seemed almost elated by the attention.

Taylor stuck her left foot in the stirrup and swung herself up and into the saddle. Her glance flickered to the rail, where Daphne and Mercedes were sitting. She noticed that the girls were talking heatedly to each other and pointing to Shafir.

Daphne nodded and got up, walking over to where Mrs. LeFleur and Keith Hobbes were standing, and gestured toward Shafir again. Mrs. LeFleur peered over her glasses and squinted, while Keith turned and asked Daphne a question, and upon receiving the response, he arched his eyebrows and crossed his arms.

Daphne rejoined Mercedes, who was now sitting talking to Eric. All three of them were immediately caught up in more animated conversation. What was going on? They were clearly discussing Shafir, but why?

Taylor shifted her attention back to the competition ring, where Plum was about to jump. Plum reached back and cracked Shafir behind her heel with the black riding crop she was holding. Shafir launched herself over the jump, a low cross-rail. The force of the motion pushed Plum back and almost out of her tack. Taylor let out a small gasp, and the crowd watched the scene intently.

Upon landing, Shafir gave a small buck. Plum tightened her grip on the reins in response, making Shafir buck again.

Taylor leaned forward, wondering what was going on with the high-spirited Arabian. Something wasn't right.

Plum pushed the sleek horse toward the next jump, a vertical. She suddenly looked rigid and tense.

Right before the jump, Shafir shied away, refusing. Plum wound up with the crop, preparing to strike.

The sudden motion caused Shafir to veer off course and gallop toward a different jump. In a panic, Shafir launched herself over first that jump, and then over another one, leaving Plum clinging to the reins. Plum pushed Shafir over one last fence and then pulled Shafir back into a trot to exit the ring.

"Rider number 194: disqualified. Off pattern," the announcer said. "Rider number 845 now entering the ring."

Taylor looked over to Plum, who had dismounted and was yelling at Shafir, thumping the horse repeatedly on the head with the palm of her hand.

Turning her attention to the task at hand, Taylor took a deep breath and clucked Prince Albert forward into the ring. She focused all she had on getting into the correct position, just as Keith had shown her. She lifted her chin, looking toward the first jump. Taylor could almost hear

Keith's voice in her head saying, "Relax! A tense rider equals a tense horse!"

Pushing Prince Albert into a canter, she approached the first jump, readying herself by moving into the jockey-like two-point, the jumping position that required her to push out of the saddle and lean closer to the horse. She placed her hands up his neck to allow Prince Albert a full range of motion as he sailed over the jump.

The thrill of jumping swept over her in an exciting wave.

Taylor couldn't hold back her joyful smile as she guided Prince Albert toward the next jump. Together they leaped over, easily clearing it. Doubling back to the next jump, a low oxer, Albert sped up with excitement. Keith had told her that a horse that was running too fast might jump lower, since the horse would straighten its neck out to go faster.

Was Prince going too fast now? Yes. Taylor began to think he was. As she tried to rein him back, she realized her efforts might be too late.

The dull clang and thud of poles being knocked over beneath them made Taylor's heart drop. Poles knocked over would result in points off, which meant no first place was possible.

Taylor rounded Prince Albert over the next few jumps, trying her hardest to remember the pattern and to keep Prince Albert under control. She couldn't let the downed poles throw her completely off. Taylor finished her pattern and exited the ring, breathing heavily from the effort. She patted Prince Albert on the neck, telling him that although it wasn't perfect, he had done a good job. She dismounted just as Daphne and Mercedes came jogging over to her.

"You did a great job!" Daphne cried, hugging Taylor.

"You, too, Prince Albert!" Mercedes chimed in, patting the black horse on the rump.

Taylor smiled gratefully. "Except for knocking down those poles on the oxer," she said, jerking her thumb back toward the ring.

Daphne waved a dismissive hand in front of her. "It was fine. Sure, you'll get a few points taken off, but you had a totally clean ride other than that." She smiled proudly at Taylor.

Taylor nodded and grinned. Suddenly remembering, she asked, "What the heck happened with Plum and Shafir? Why was she acting up so badly?"

Mercedes' expression changed from a happy smile to one of extreme exasperation. "That fool was using a double twisted wire snaffle on Shafir. That kind of bit is very severe and should only be used on very large, strong horses, like draft horses, or by very experienced riders," Mercedes explained. "It's definitely not for using on a mostly green, flighty Arabian. That's why Shafir was acting so weird — because Plum was yanking on her face with a tough bit. She thought that just because it had the word *snaffle* in it, it was fine."

Taylor's jaw hung open. "Really? Poor Shafir! Is she okay?"

Daphne shrugged but then gave a small nod. "She'll be fine eventually. But Shafir's mouth was bleeding."

Taylor gasped.

"Don't worry, though," Daphne added. "Keith Hobbes gave her a very stern talking to about choosing the correct bit. She won't be making any more mistakes like that, I'm sure."

"Good to hear it," Taylor said. "I think that —" Taylor was cut off by a pat on the back from behind her. She whirled around and came face-to-face with Eric.

"Great work!" Eric said, smiling broadly. "You looked

awesome! Did you see what happened to Plum out there? I couldn't tell what was going wrong."

Normally, this sort of attention from Eric would have made her heart melt. Now, she didn't know how to feel. Had he lied to her about where his friend was getting all of this stuff? She didn't know what she would do if she found out that his friend and he had been lying and stealing. It would totally change her view of Eric forever.

"Yeah, maybe it wouldn't have been so bad if Plum didn't have that *new* bit in his mouth. The one from your *friend*," she said starkly, and turned away from him, marching toward the trailer.

A moment later Taylor heard Eric hurrying after her and then felt his hand on her shoulder.

"Whoa, wait, what's wrong with you? What are you so mad about?" he asked, brows furrowed with concern. She whirled around to look him in the eyes.

"Nothing," she snapped.

"Come on, tell me," Eric urged her. "Something's bugging you."

"Eric, you didn't . . . I mean, you wouldn't . . ." How could she ask this question? She couldn't just blurt out that she thought he might be a thief. It was so insulting!

"I wouldn't what?" Eric questioned.

"Those things we got from your friend," Taylor began.

"Yeah, what about them?"

She just couldn't bring herself to ask him. "It's nothing. We'll talk about this later, okay?"

Desperate to get away from this awkward and unhappy confrontation, Taylor walked off, leading Prince Albert. She headed toward the trailer and began to untack the gelding, not daring to look back to where Eric stood.

Taylor had taken off Prince Albert's saddle and was undoing his girth when Eric came alongside her again. Prince Albert shifted uncomfortably but stayed put. As long as Eric didn't touch him, Taylor hoped her horse wouldn't act up.

"Why didn't you wait for the results?" Eric asked.

"They announced them already?" Taylor asked, surprised.

"Yeah, they just did. You won third place!"

Taylor gasped. "Really? Third place!"

He smiled at her. "Yeah!"

Taylor's jaw dropped as his words sank in. Third place was not bad at all — especially considering that she was a new jumper.

"Way to go!" Eric cheered. He hugged her happily. "Now will you tell me why you're so mad?"

"All right," Taylor agreed. "I don't want you to be insulted, but I'm just going to come out and ask you a question. Are the horse things you gave me stolen?"

Eric took a step back, his eyes wide with surprise. "What?"

Taylor told him about the detectives and what they'd said.

"No, I swear! I believed the guy's story. I thought he was selling me stuff the store was throwing out anyway," Eric insisted. "I'm not kidding. I would never do something like that."

Did she believe him? He seemed to be sincerely shocked by her news. But could she be sure?

"Taylor, you don't believe me, do you?" Eric said, looking hurt. "I can see it on your face."

"I just don't know, Eric," Taylor admitted. "I mean . . . you said the guy was a friend of yours. How could you not realize what he was doing? If he was your friend, wouldn't he tell you?"

"He's not really a *friend*. He's just a guy I know from around town."

Taylor so wanted to believe him. But if she did, would she just be fooling herself? Would she be making excuses for Eric?

"I don't know what I should think," Taylor admitted to him. "I'm so confused."

"Did you tell the police you got the things from me?" Eric asked.

"No."

"Why not?" he demanded.

Taylor shrugged. "I wasn't sure what to do. I didn't want you to get in trouble."

Eric's brows knit into an unhappy V. "Then you do think I'm guilty," he said, turning away from her.

"I just didn't know for cert —"

Taylor cut her words short as Eric walked away angrily.

Chapter 15

Taylor closed her eyes and laid her head back against the front seat of the horse trailer, with her third-place ribbon in her lap, thinking about the day's events. She was glad for the quiet — Plum was silent in the backseat, and everyone else had gotten other rides back — but she couldn't stop picturing Eric's hurt expression when they'd talked. The look on his face had been sincere. In her heart and in her gut, she thought he was innocent. Everything she knew about him told her that Eric would never steal or lie.

And besides, Prince Albert had allowed Eric to ride him. Taylor trusted her horse's instincts — maybe even more than she trusted her own. It didn't matter if Eric had been wearing her scarf. Taylor believed that if there was something essentially dishonest in Eric's nature, Prince Albert would never have allowed him to ride.

Plum scowled out the window into the darkness while Mrs. LeFleur drove. Taylor wondered if she'd learned anything at all from what had happened that day. Would she treat Shafir more gently now? Had she learned to be more careful when she groomed and tacked up the lively mare? Or would she only ride Shafir harder than ever and treat her even more harshly because she was angry about the horse's performance in the ring? Taylor really hoped not.

When they pulled into Wildwood Stables, Taylor spied Mrs. Mason's car idling off to the side of the main building. Mrs. LeFleur drove up to the front and cut the engine. Without even a word of good-bye, Plum got out and headed toward her mother's car and got in. When she was inside, she lowered her window. "Eric!" Plum shouted. "Hurry up. We're giving you a lift home."

"Give me one minute, okay?"

Taylor followed the sound of his voice and noticed a car belonging to Daphne's father. Mr. Chang and Daphne stood on one side of the car with Eric. They were excitedly discussing something.

Taylor noticed an unfamiliar car parked at the corner of the main building. When she saw the passengers inside it, Taylor drew a sharp, alarmed breath.

"What is it?" Mrs. LeFleur asked.

"Mercedes' mother is here," Taylor said, pointing to a car parked next to the Changs'. "That must be a new car she's bought since the other was wrecked in the accident."

Mercedes sat in the front seat beside her mother. The two of them were engaged in a serious conversation. Taylor was worried. Had Mrs. Gonzalez somehow discovered that Mercedes was coming here? Mercedes was probably in big trouble right now. Was this the last time Taylor would ever see her here at Wildwood?

"Why do you find Mrs. Gonzalez's appearance so upsetting?" Mrs. LeFleur asked as she came to a stop.

Taylor suddenly remembered that Mrs. LeFleur wasn't aware that Mrs. Gonzalez had forbidden Mercedes to come to the ranch. Taylor quickly filled her in. "Oh, dear," Mrs. LeFleur said as she got out of the trailer.

Taylor hurried after her as Mrs. LeFleur approached the group. "Hello, Mrs. Gonzalez," Mrs. LeFleur greeted her. "How are you healing?" she asked with a nod at the foot-to-knee cast the woman wore below her skirt.

Mrs. Gonzalez was an elegant-looking woman with dark hair and a stylish way of dressing. Taylor didn't particularly like her haughty demeanor and usually found her intimidating.

"I should be out of this cast in another few weeks," Mrs. Gonzalez reported evenly. "I've brought the papers that Mrs. Ross said you needed, the ones for Montana Wind Dancer." She stretched out her arm to offer the papers.

"Mrs. Ross said I need them?" Mrs. LeFleur inquired. "Whatever for?"

Mrs. Gonzalez looked confused. "She said she wants to start using Monty on the circuit, and she wants Mercedes to work with her, along with your son, Jim. Didn't she tell you all this?"

Taylor swung around to look at Mercedes. One look at the girl's beaming, radiant expression told Taylor that everything Mrs. Gonzalez had said was true.

"And you don't mind Mercedes being here?" Mrs. LeFleur asked cautiously.

"Not anymore," Mrs. Gonzalez said. "Mercedes called me from the horse show and asked me to meet her here. She just now admitted to me that she had been coming to Wildwood on the sneak. Don't worry. She explained that you were unaware I had forbidden her to come."

"I had no idea," Mrs. LeFleur confirmed.

"I had to admit I'd been coming here," Mercedes explained. "It was the only way I could talk to Mom about Monty."

"And she's grounded, by the way," Mrs. Gonzalez added. "I don't like her lying to me like that."

"For how long?" Taylor dared to ask.

"Till I say so," Mrs. Gonzalez replied as Mercedes stared humbly down at her shoes. "But I'm glad my daughter was finally honest with me. She told me how much this place means to her, how she thinks of it as the best place in the world."

"It is," Taylor agreed.

"I spoke with Mrs. Ross on the phone the other night, and she told me how she had seen Mercedes with Monty at the Ross River show last month and realized what a bond the two of them had," Mrs. Gonzalez went on. "She wants to use Monty on the riding circuit and thinks Mercedes is just the girl to work with her. I couldn't say no. I understand how much Mercedes loves Monty."

"Then Plum isn't going to buy him?" Taylor blurted, as she cast a quick glance over at Plum, relieved to see that Plum had once again closed her window.

Mercedes lowered her voice. "She wanted to but Mrs. Ross refused. She's heard about Plum's reputation with horses."

Taylor recalled hearing that Ross River had refused to lease horses to Plum anymore after one of their horses had died under Plum's harsh treatment. Taylor had to give Mrs. Ross or her barn manager credit for that decision.

"You will let Mercedes work with Monty here at the ranch, won't you, Mrs. LeFleur?" Daphne said hopefully.

Everyone stared expectantly at Wildwood's owner. "I hadn't planned to," Mrs. LeFleur told them. "My cousin Devon was here the other day to inquire about it."

Taylor realized it was the first time Mrs. LeFleur had referred to Devon Ross by her first name, or even admitted that they were cousins. Did she detect a slight thaw in their icy feud?

"And what did you tell her?" Daphne asked.

"I was going to tell her no," Mrs. LeFleur revealed.

Mercedes, Daphne, and Taylor all gasped at once.

Mrs. LeFleur smiled. "But look at you all! Mercedes wants it so much, and you both want it for her. How could I ever say no?"

Mercedes leaped in the air and ran to hug Mrs. LeFleur. Then she whirled around and wrapped her mother in a tight hug, as well. Taylor could see that there were tears of joy in her friend's eyes. She was about to be reunited with her beloved Monty.

Approaching from behind them, Taylor came up alongside Eric. He had moved away from Daphne and her father and was now standing alone. Taylor reached out and gently touched his elbow to get his attention. "Don't be angry," she said. "I'm sorry I thought you had anything to do with stealing that stuff."

"I didn't. You have to believe me. I didn't know."

"I believe you," Taylor said sincerely.

"I'll call the police tonight and tell them what I know. That guy lied to me. I don't owe him any loyalty."

Nodding in agreement, Taylor smiled at Eric. He smiled back just as Plum came walking up. Ignoring Taylor, Plum pulled Eric toward Beverly Mason's car for his ride home. Eric grinned at Taylor apologetically as he allowed himself to be dragged off.

With a last wave to him, Taylor went around to the back of the trailer and opened it. Boosting herself up, she went to Prince Albert. Taylor laid her forehead on the side of his neck and stroked his side. "You were wonderful today, boy," she praised him. She took the third-place ribbon from the inside pocket of her denim jacket. "This is yours, too," she told him. "It's our third ribbon together. Who would have ever thought it?"

Prince Albert neighed and Taylor patted him. These wonderful things could only be happening here at Wildwood Stables — the best place in the world.

Come back to

WILDWOOD STABLES

Taking the Leap

Turn the page for a sneak peek!

Pay attention to your diagonals," Keith Hobbes reminded thirteen-year-old Taylor Henry as she cantered around the indoor ring at Ross River Ranch. The renowned riding instructor stood in the center of the ring with his arms folded, watching. He was dressed as always in a black T-shirt, tan breeches, and polished black tall boots. He pushed back his brimmed cap revealing tufts of white hair.

Taylor struggled to recall what Keith had taught her about diagonals. A confident rider in Western style, she was new to English riding.

What was it he'd taught her during their last session? Slowing to a trot, Taylor tried to remember.

When she was traveling clockwise in a ring, as she was at that moment, then the correct diagonal was the outside diagonal. This meant that her horse's left front leg and her right back leg were both supposed to be forward at the same time.

Was she on the correct diagonal now? Taylor wasn't sure.

Taylor stopped posting and sat into the saddle. She checked the shoulder of the mare she was riding. Serafina, a black quarter horse with a white blaze, belonged to Ross River Ranch. The horse's shoulder was forward, which wasn't what Taylor wanted.

To get onto the correct diagonal, Taylor would have to change position. But how?

Then she remembered what Keith had told her to do. To get her posting into the correct sit-rise-sit rhythm, she sat for an extra beat and then rose into the post as soon as Serafina's shoulder went back.

"That's it!" Keith encouraged her. "Good girl!"

Taylor beamed at her instructor, proud of earning his approval. She had so much respect for Keith, a retired United States Equestrian Federation judge, an A circuit competitor, and a former Olympic dressage team trainer. Winning these free lessons was one of the best things that had ever happened to her. On her own, she could never have afforded to train with him.

A lithe, willowy girl with silky long black hair entered the spectator area outside of the ring. Taylor, recognizing the girl immediately, waved and smiled.

Daphne Chang was the sixteen-year-old instructor

over at Wildwood Stables. She boarded her gray speckled mare, Mandy, across the aisle from Taylor's black quarter horse gelding, Prince Albert, and Pixie, the cream Shetland pony mare. Taylor had acquired Prince Albert and Pixie in a rescue and now worked for their board at the newly opened, rustic ranch.

Daphne returned Taylor's wave, but she didn't smile as Taylor would have expected her to. Taylor's brow furrowed in worried confusion. What was wrong with Daphne?

"Okay, Taylor, that's enough for today," Keith called as he approached Daphne with a friendly smile. "Nice job."

"Thanks!" Taylor hadn't realized Daphne knew Keith but remembered that Daphne had boarded Mandy at Ross River before bring the barb-Arabian mix over to Wildwood. That was probably how she knew Keith.

Taylor slowed Serafina to a walk to let her cool down before bringing her back to be groomed by the ranch's stable hands. These stables were so different from Wildwood, where all riders did their own grooming and tacking. Everything was luxurious at Ross River Ranch.

Trying not to be too obvious, Taylor cut her eyes over to where Daphne sat with Keith. They were in a deep discussion. Then they both stood and shook hands.

Keith left, exiting to the outside. Daphne stood and waited as Taylor approached, riding Serafina at a walk. "What was that about?" Taylor asked.

"Keith asked me to be his assistant," Daphne revealed, not meeting Taylor's eyes.

"That's great!" Taylor cried. "That's wonderful. Congratulations. There's no one better than Keith. You'll learn so much. Not that you need to."

"Are you kidding?" Daphne replied. "I definitely have a lot to learn about training and instructing. To work with Keith Hobbes is the chance of a lifetime."

"Is he going to pay you a lot?" Taylor asked.

"The pay is excellent, plus free board for Mandy."

Taylor blinked, not quite understanding. "Board? But you already board her at Wildwood."

"But this would be free, and it's so much nicer here."

"Are you saying you would leave Wildwood Stables?"

"It's a great opportunity," Daphne replied, a defensive note in her voice.

"But you'll still give lessons at Wildwood, won't you?" Taylor asked, growing concerned.

"I might not be able to," Daphne replied, looking away.

You belong at
WILDWOOD STABLES

Daring to Dream

Taylor Henry loves horses, but her single mom can't afford riding lessons, much less a horse. So when she discovers an abandoned gelding and pony, Taylor is happy just to be around them.

But the rescued animals have nowhere to go, and Taylor is running out of time to find them a good home. Could the empty old barn on Wildwood Lane be the answer? And could Taylor's wildest dream—of a horse to call her own—finally be coming true?

Playing for Keeps

Taylor Henry thinks
Wildwood Stables is
perfect—even if it needs
repair and a lot more
money, it's become a
home to her and her
new horse, Prince
Albert. And as soon as Taylor trains Prince
Albert to give lessons, Wildwood will be in business!

But the gelding refuses to let anyone ride him except
Taylor. Can she convince Prince Albert to earn his keep?
Or will Taylor need the help of her worst enemy to save
her beloved new home?

Racing Against Time

Taylor Henry and her
horse, Prince Albert,
are really settling in at
Wildwood Stables. Prince Albert has even
become a valuable therapy horse for a young girl with autism.

There's just one problem: Spoiled Plum Mason is always
at Wildwood, too. Worse, she's overtraining her new horse,
Shafir. Can Taylor and the other Wildwood girls keep Shafir
safe? Or will Plum's suspiciously bad luck with horses strike
again?

Learning to Fly

Taylor Henry is finally learning English-style riding, just in time for elite Ross River Ranch's jumping competition. The grand prize is free riding lessons, and Taylor has her eye on the prize!

But it won't be a smooth ride to victory. Plum Mason is also entering the show, competing in Taylor's division. And learning to jump is much harder than Taylor had expected! It's time to take the reins—and a big leap of faith.

Read them all!